Indecent Temptations

Viktor Redreich

Redreich Publishing Limited

Free Book

Get your free book now

https://redreich.com/dirtysecrets

Published by Redreich Publishing Limited

71-75 Shelton Street, Covent Garden London WC2H 9JQ United Kingdom

Contents

Introduction

This story takes place in a small town in Scotland.

It has been written in a slightly Scottish version of English.

The grammar may not be what you're used to.

Try reading it in a Scottish accent if you can.

Chapter One

Stop flirting with dads

"You know, if I'd had a teacher as pretty as you, I don't think I would have had any trouble with my studies."

I smiled at the man who had just delivered what he, no doubt, thought was the smoothest line in the book. Damien was a few years younger than me, always made a point to chat me up, and might have been the sort of guy I'd have let buy me a drink, if I was already a couple deep. And, as he lingered outside the school waiting to pick up his daughter, I supposed now was as good a time as any to practice my flirting skills.

"Maybe you could tell some of my students that," I joked back lightly.

I knew that I should have been a little more stringent about shutting down the attentions of the sweet, flirty dads who stopped by the school to pick up their kids, but I was allowed to indulge in a little flirtation every now and then, wasn't I? I had been doing this for long enough to know where the line was, and I never took it too far – just far enough to give both our egos a little boost, and to make sure that they would *never* miss a teacher's night meeting with me.

"I'm not sure they'd take it from an old fart like me," he replied, and I cocked my head at him.

"I must have a few years on you," I protested. "What does that make me, if you're old?"

"Mature," he replied, and he let his gaze slip down over the outfit I was wearing – but before he could say anything else, a car door slammed behind him and a woman emerged to lean next to him on the peeling green paint of the old gate that cut the school off from the rest of the world.

She had a baby strapped to her chest, a pencil stabbed through a bun in her hair, and she put her hand on his shoulder at once, staking her claim on him. I didn't need telling twice. I could read woman-code for *please don't make me feel bad about myself by flirting with my husband right in front of me,* and I figured it was the least I could do to respect it.

"Anyway, I should get in and make sure we haven't got any stragglers left," I remarked, smiling at Damien and nodding to his wife. And with that, I headed back inside the building before I got plastered with the title of homewrecker, over a guy who I had only really been flirting with out of politeness, anyway.

In a small community in northeast Scotland like this one, rumors spread fast and stuck faster. I taught at the small school of Crainlioch, a blended high school and primary that served the inhabitants of the sparse and spackled local community. Most of them came down from the old crofter's houses in the hills, but others were closer to the Loch, living in little clusters of homes that filled out the frigid banks with life.

I lived in the coastal city of Inverness. I couldn't cope with life out here in the middle of nowhere, though sometimes Inverness felt like it might as well have been that. It purported to be a city, but I wasn't sure I believed it, not when it still had the same feel as these tiny little rural clusters. I had moved out there from Drumnadrochit, home to the famed Loch Ness Monster, in the hopes that I would find a little more life, but it hadn't served me as well as I had hoped.

I stepped back into the old stone school building that I spent most of my days inside – it was strange, from the outside, it looked like it could have been in a period drama, but within the walls it was as modern and average as any other school, all scuffed parquet floors and coat-hooks with little animals next to them so that the younger kids would remember where to leave their belongings.

My classroom would probably have looked tiny next to one in Edinburgh or Glasgow – I taught the whole of the second-year high school student class here, and there were only a couple of dozen of them to speak of. Still, I liked the smallness of it. I liked having the chance to get to know everyone I taught. I felt like I had a solid connection with them, and that was such a big reason as to why I had chosen to teach here instead of one of the schools in the city. That, and my loose, slightly hippy-ish style fit in better here than it did in places of a more urban nature.

It was quiet when I closed the door behind me, and I took a moment to close my eyes and take in the peace. I had seen off the class for the weekend, and I'd been on gate duty to count the lot of them out. Now that I was all done, I felt like I could relax. Not that I had ever actually been much good at that.

I couldn't stop thinking about Damien. Not that I actually wanted anything to do with him – no, he was too young for me, and he was married, and a little awkward, and had a scar where he'd been hit with a shinty stick as a kid that made his eyes look a little squint. But I was thinking about his wife. And the fact that she had actually managed to find someone, while I was still out here wandering around like the old spinster of the hills, wondering if I was ever going to catch someone who made me feel like I could spend a lifetime with them.

I supposed this had been on my mind a lot since Eilidh had gotten married.

Eilidh, my younger sister. She had always been the pretty one out of the two of us – I think even she would have agreed with me on that one – and when she had gone off to Edinburgh to study Gaelic translation, she had been inundated with men who wanted to make her their one and only. She had eventually settled down with Lukas, a Polish transplant who worked for the government, and the two of them had finally tied the knot just a few months before.

It didn't seem fair that my younger sister should be getting married before me. That wasn't the way it was meant to work, was it? I was meant to be all settled down, offering sage advice on the business of being a wife to anyone who needed it, and yet here I was, still unwed, still wondering if there was anyone I hadn't already gone out on a flunked date with at some point in the surrounding area.

"You'll find someone, you will," Eilidh had told me when I had gotten a little tipsy at her bachelorette party. "You're a catch."

"Then why has nobody popped the question yet?" I asked, trying to keep my tone jovial, but finding that it sounded more whiny when I said it out loud.

"I honestly have no idea," Eilidh admitted. "I thought you and Lewis were meant to be, but..."

She must have seen me wince because she dropped that line of questioning before it went any further. She knew that bringing up Lewis to me was just asking for trouble. The memory of him still stung, no matter how much I would have liked to pretend that I was totally and cheerfully over everything about him.

Ugh. Even thinking about him now made my heart sink. I had thought the same as her – I had assumed that it was just a matter of time before he asked me to marry him. Maybe he would have, if it hadn't been for...

No, I couldn't let myself think about that. Now wasn't the time. It was too heavy for me to let it cross my mind on a Friday night, when I was meant to be having fun. If I was going to go out and meet someone, then I would need to go to the pub with a smile on my face, not heaving the baggage of my past out with me.

And God only knew how much I wanted to meet someone.

I knew it was hardly the most feminist outlook on life, but I wanted a man – I wanted a husband, a family. I was thirty-eight years old, and I felt like time was running out for me to meet someone who really worked for me; I felt like, soon enough, I was just going to have to take what I could get, and hope that any man I came across would be alright dealing with the fact that I...

"Well, T-G-I-Friday!" Mallory exclaimed as she wandered into my classroom. I instantly pushed the thoughts that had been plaguing me to the back of my mind – I knew that Mallory would never let me think about myself in that way. She had been my biggest cheerleader since we had started working together three years before. Even though she had only just turned thirty, we had a lot in common, and I was always glad to see her burst into my room with no warning.

"Agreed," I replied, and I put a smile on my face. She kept little mini-bottles of wine in the drawer at her desk that we sometimes indulged in if it had been a particularly tough week. I could have used one of those tonight – might make me feel a little less sorry for myself.

"How's your week been?" She asked. "I feel like I've hardly seen you."

"End-of-term, though, right?" I pointed out to her. "Not long till we'll be able to sit by the river drinking rosé and pretending that we've never had to mark a paper in our lives."

"And in what teacher-training-free world is this little vignette taking place in?" She asked curiously. I laughed. She had a point. Even with the summer coming up, it wasn't like we just got to put our feet up for seven weeks.

"Paula and I were thinking about heading down to the Hunter's for a drink this evening," she told me. "I was thinking you could probably use a break, too?"

I pondered on the proposal for a moment. It would have been nice to get a little tipsy and forget about my troubles for a while, but in truth, I didn't feel like the trek back to my flat in Inverness when it was all over and done with. Much as I loved spending time with Mallory and our other friends on the faculty, I was feeling a little maudlin and wanted nothing more than some time to myself.

"I think I should probably just get the last of my marking done and then head home," I replied, and she narrowed her eyes at me and planted her hands on her hips.

"Did something happen?" She asked, always able to see through me like she had X-vision. I shook my head.

"No, I'm just tired," I lied. "And I have some errands to run tomorrow, I don't want to have a hangover..."

"Who said we're going to be drinking enough to be hungover?" She protested, and I tipped my head to the side and raised my eyebrows at her.

"Sorry, did I hear you wrong? I thought you said you were going to the Hunter's," I reminded her. "And I've been with you on enough of those nights to know how they end."

"Oh, don't act like I haven't had to bundle you into a taxi home while you were trying to get me to sing Loch Lomond with you," she teased me. I held my hands up.

"Hey, never said I didn't," I agreed. "But I don't feel like it tonight, that's all. I'll catch you some other time, alright?"

"Alright," she replied. "But you give me a text if you need some company over the weekend, won't you? I don't like the thought of you sitting around at home by yourself for the next couple of days..."

"Really? Because I think it sounds like a treat," I replied.

"Any chance to get away from me, eh?" Mallory responded.

"You've rumbled me," I agreed, and I grabbed my bag from where I had hooked it over my desk chair.

"I'll see you on Monday then, alright?" She suggested. "I think it's my turn to bring in the coffees."

"I think it is," I agreed, and she put an arm around my waist and led me out into the grounds once more; half of the playground was covered with tarmac and sketched out with hopscotch lines and chalk designs, and the other was taken up with a muddy, slightly hilly grass area that was used to conduct football tournaments every single lunchtime.

I gave Mal a hug at the gate and said goodbye, and then climbed into my car and started the drive back up into the city. It had just started to rain by the time I passed over the bridge and into town once more, and the River Ness was speckled with the ripples of raindrops on the water. And there I was, thinking that it was meant to be summer sometime soon. Maybe I had blinked and missed it.

I got back to my small flat just off the River and sighed as soon as the door clicked shut behind me. The place was dark and cool and I wished I had someone there to greet me as I came through the door. Someone who could put the heating on while I was out. Order a takeaway for us to cuddle up on the couch and enjoy together. I kicked off my canvas shoes and tossed them into the hallway, then flopped down onto the couch.

It wasn't that I just wanted *a* man. I wasn't in my twenties anymore, and I wasn't going to settle for whoever came through the door just so I could keep up with my friends and not feel left behind. I wanted someone who made me feel *alive.* Who made me feel like I could take on the world. Or at least, take on a family. A partner. A real partner. That was what I needed. No boys, no boyfriends, but a partner, someone who could stand by my side and would do everything they could to protect me against the world, while supporting me on my way through it.

But where was I going to find one of those? Sure as hell not standing at the gate of the school waiting for his wife, or down at the familiar stools of the Hunter's Inn. I needed to think bigger. I needed to think newer. And I...

I needed to think about this in the morning, once I'd gotten some sleep. Then, I could get around to changing my life.

Yeah, in the morning.

Chapter Two

Red lipstick vixen

"OH MY GOD, I can't believe how close we are to being done right now," Mallory murmured to me, keeping her voice low to make sure that she didn't tip off any of the parents around us to the fact that we were counting down the minutes till term ended.

"I know," I agreed, grinning at her and glancing at my watch. "Twenty minutes? And then it's all done."

"Until we have to come back in for teacher training," she replied, pulling a face. I pulled one right back.

"But we can pretend that we're on holiday for a little while, can't we?" I pointed out. "Even just tonight?"

"If you're inviting me out for a drink, then consider this an acceptance," she replied. I opened my mouth to protest, but then closed it again. God only knew how much I needed a drink to take the edge off the last few days of term.

All the kids just got totally lazy and it was hard to get them to do anything other than talk about their holiday plans or maybe watch a movie if we could manage to get them all in one room long enough. Now, as everyone cleared out their trays and grabbed their stuff, it was obvious that their minds were a million miles away. Some of them literally; I had heard a few of the girls talking about the family trips they were taking to Spain or France, and I would have been lying if I'd said that I wasn't more than a little jealous. I couldn't really afford to go anywhere, even with my limited holiday weeks, given that all of my money mostly went into paying for that little flat of mine.

All the families were clustered around the front gate, ready to scoop up their collection of kids and head off into the next seven weeks without any school to bother them. I knew that for some parents, this would be a dream come true – a lot of them really did miss their kids like crazy in the time that they were away. For others, it would just be a scheduling nightmare, a signal that they would have to try to find some way to balance their work and their kids and their lives for a couple of months without losing their minds.

It would have been easy for me, if I'd had a family. My time off would have lined up with theirs. Whoever I had them with, they wouldn't have to take any time off work. It would have been perfect.

If I'd had kids. If I even *could* have kids.

It was hard not to get a little melancholy on days like this when I saw the families together and wondered what my life could have been like if I'd been able to connect to one of my own over the years. I knew that it was going to be hard, given that I didn't exactly have the ability to create them myself, but there had to be someone out there who was willing to see all that I had to give and would want to give me a shot, despite my issues.

But I didn't want to take someone who came along and looked at me and said *yeah, sure, I guess.* I wanted someone who was going to be committed to me for me and not anything else. Committed to making a future with me, to building a family. When I looked at the men, those fathers and husbands clustered around the school gate, I felt a jolt of sureness run through my system. They had made that choice. They had seen the woman they loved and decided to make a future with her. It wasn't totally crazy to think that someone could look at me and think the same thing, was it?

The end of term caused introspection – I supposed it was the same whenever anything came to a close, but this felt like something particular had shifted, something that I was struggling to get a hold on. Did I really want to come back after the holidays and find that nothing had changed in me? Did I want to be the same version of myself that I was right now? Because that version, that version of me hadn't been enough – it hadn't come close to enough, not for anyone. I needed to step things up. I needed to get out there.

I needed to prove to myself that there was nothing that was holding me back.

"What are you thinking about?" Mallory asked, as she brushed past me with an armful of papers to take to the recycling. I shook my head.

"Just looking forward to that drink tonight," I replied. "That's all."

And I was – I did my make-up in the primary school bathrooms because I knew that they would be quiet already, given the half-day that those kids had been given. It wasn't often that I took the time to put an actual face on, given that I was just presenting to a bunch of teenagers who tried to actively avoid looking me in the eye if they could help it.

But tonight felt different somehow; tonight, I found myself wanting to do something a little different.

Even though it was the same pub, and the same crowd, and the same Mallory coming along with me, maybe I could switch it up to some new version of myself.

I had no idea what the new me looked like or what she felt like or how she would move through the world, but I had to give her a shot, didn't I? I had been hiding her away for a long time now, whoever she was, and maybe her different approach was what I needed.

I put on some dark red lipstick, wiped it off, and then put it on again. Yes. Maybe this version of me could be a vixen. Maybe she could be sexy. Maybe she could *own* that sexiness. I was still wearing a long, flowing brocade skirt and a peasant blouse, but it was all about the attitude that you projected, wasn't it? Not just the outfit.

"Damn!" Mallory exclaimed, fanning herself when she set eyes on me. "Lady in red over here. You out on the pull?"

"No, I don't think so," I replied. "Just feel like getting a little dressed up, that's all. We're celebrating, aren't we?"

"Damn right we are," Mallory agreed, and she hooked her arm through mine; she had changed into a pair of dark, tight jeans and a cute, slouchy t-shirt that showed off her flat tummy and small, delicate frame. She was young, she could still get away with just throwing on whatever and looking hot as hell. I couldn't get away with that anymore...

Or maybe I just *thought* I couldn't. Perhaps it was the believing in the thing that made it true. I tried to lock that thought into my head as we left the cleaners to scrub down the school, and made it out to the pub for the first drink of the night.

The place was half-full, mostly of the usual locals; it was, to them, just another Thursday night, but to us, it was a chance to actually kick back and relax after putting the chaos of the term behind us. It had been a crazy-busy last few days, and honestly, a cheap glass of wine or three was already calling my name.

"To actually getting some time to ourselves," Mallory toasted to me, and I touched my glass to her's.

"*Slange Var,"* I replied, and she grinned and took a sip of her white wine. She had been a party girl when she had been down in Glasgow, she'd told me, and man, she could still drink enough to make me believe it.

"So, what are you going to do for the next couple of weeks?" I asked. "Before we have to go back in for training?"

"I am going to lie very fucking still on my couch and nothing is going to be able to move me," she replied, and she clasped her hands to her chest dramatically.

"Oh, it feels so good to actually be able to swear again," she groaned. "I've been biting back all the *fucks* for the last couple of weeks, but I don't have to worry about it anymore. I'd forgotten how much fun it was."

"So you're going to be lying on your couch reciting every swear word you've ever heard before?" I asked, and she nodded.

"That's the plan," she agreed, taking another sip of her drink. "Maybe going down to see my family in Glasgow for a few days, I'm not sure yet. And what about you? How are you spending the summer?"

I bit my lip. I didn't want to tell her about my plans, just in case they didn't come through. There was nothing worse than talking a big talk and then having to take it all back a few months later when you realized that you couldn't deliver on any of it. Besides, I knew that if I even hinted to Mallory that I wanted to change things up, she would have come sliding right in there to make it her mission to interfere with what I was planning to do. She was a good friend to me, the best I could have asked for, but I knew that I needed to do this on my own terms. The thought of letting anyone else in on this was just...yeah, it was far too scary. Even though I knew I was going to have to, sooner or later.

"Nothing, really," I replied. "Just trying to get some rest and forget that the rest of the year is coming up, you know?"

"I feel that," she agreed, and she touched her glass to mine once more and glanced around the room.

"Could use a new someone to take the edge off, though," she remarked, as cool and calm as she ever was when it came to talking about men. She was happily and utterly single, and seemed to have no intention of changing that anytime soon. Sometimes, I wished that I could have taken on her level of remove about the whole situation. It would surely be better than spending all my time twisting and turning inside my own head as I tried to figure out what I was meant to be doing with my life.

"I don't think you're going to find anyone new here," I pointed out with a chuckle. The upside of coming here every time we wanted a drink was that the guy behind the bar always knew what to pour us; the downside was that it was about the worst place possible to meet new people, given that we knew almost everyone who came in and out of here.

"I don't know, look at them," she replied, and I glanced around to see where she was looking. Sure enough, there were a couple of guys sitting at the bar that I hadn't seen before. They were younger than us, even younger than Mallory, but they were stealing glances in our direction like they could hardly believe their luck at having found us.

"They're practically teenagers," I protested, and Mallory cocked her head to the side and hit me with a hard look.

"And? They're obviously over eighteen if they're drinking here..."

"Some of the kids at the school are nearly eighteen," I reminded her, and she waved her hand.

"Come on, you can see they're older than that," she pointed out. "Look at them. They're men, not boys. And they're checking us out. Why don't we invite them over here and we can see what they've got going on? Worst that happens is that we get a free round out of this."

"Fine," I replied. "But don't act like you're trying to set me up, alright? I'm not looking to get together with boys that young."

"Oh, come on, it's just a little flirtation," she replied, and she turned to face the two of them and offered them a broad smile. The younger one, his face all but actually lit up when he saw her looking at him. I couldn't help but laugh. She just had this effect on men, it seemed. I would have been jealous, but those weren't exactly the kind of men that I was out here trying to attract. I doubted the two of them had given any thought to their futures. Well, the futures that went beyond the hangovers that they were going to be dealing with tomorrow morning, that was for sure.

They joined us at the table, pulling around extra chairs so that they could sit, and Mallory tossed her hair over her shoulder and smiled at them both.

"So, what brings you here?" She asked. "Looks like you're new in town."

"Yeah, we're traveling through for a gig," One of them, the younger-looking one, replied. "Not staying for long. I suppose you are regulars here?"

"Something like that," Mallory agreed. "I'm Mallory, this is Abi. We teach at the school not far from here."

"Oh, teachers, huh?" The other one cut in. "Not going to get us in trouble for not doing our homework, are you?"

"That depends," Mallory replied. "On whether you'd be willing to get the next round or not..."

"Come show me what you take," The younger one told her, and they got up and headed to the bar, leaving me and this young man sitting there facing each other. He smiled at me.

"I'm Matt," he introduced himself. "And don't worry, I'm not going to embarrass myself by trying to put the moves on you."

"Why not?" I replied without thinking, and I felt an instant flush run up my neck. I tried to cool it off. I had to be a little more gathered, a little more together if I was going to sell myself as some desirable, sexy woman. Even though I had no intention of going anywhere with this boy tonight, I could at least use him for a little flirtation.

"Your friend seemed a little chattier," he remarked, and he shifted forward on his seat to get a little closer to me. "I thought you might just be going along with this."

"Well, maybe I haven't decided yet," I replied, cocking an eyebrow. He grinned. I smiled back. Something about the red lipstick had me feeling some type of way, and I could feel that flutter in the base of my belly, the flutter of knowing that this man wanted me, that he desired me. It had been a long time since I had allowed anyone to make me feel that way, and for good reason – it was normally too dangerous for me to think about letting anyone else anywhere near me, not after what had happened with my ex. But here, I was in control. I was calling the shots. And that meant that if I wanted to flirt, I would damn well flirt a little.

Mallory and her man headed back to the table, and I noticed that she was already pressing herself up against him a little – she was clearly already a little cheerful, and I couldn't blame her. Spending all that time around kids all day made it hard, occasionally, to remember what it was like to strike out into the world and be an adult. She was clearly ready to remember. And maybe I was, too.

The rest of the night, I was surprised to find, was pretty fun. It had been a long time since I had just allowed myself to flirt with someone for the fun of it, but I flirted with Matt like my life depended on it, and I found myself having a good time. I made it pretty clear that I wasn't interested in going home with him and he was totally cool about that, apparently, like me, just enjoying the attention that came from a stranger in a pub who didn't hold any preconceptions about you and just wanted to have a good time. I got a little tipsy but not too drunk, and kept an eye on Mallory to make sure she was staying the fun side of boozy.

By the time that the night drew to a close, she was practically hanging off the arm of her man, Callum, and they were clearly all ready to head home together. I didn't begrudge her the good time; in fact, I was glad for her, that she still seemed so able to cut loose and have fun like that without thinking about the kind of person she wanted to settle down with. I hugged her goodbye, and Matt walked me to the cab that I had called to pick me up outside.

"Thanks for the drinks," I told him, and he shook his head.

"Thanks for the company," he replied. "You did us a solid. Don't know how we would have entertained ourselves if we hadn't met you."

The cab pulled up, and I glanced over at it; I knew that the night was over, and I was more than ready to get home. I had been blessed with a guy who didn't seem too pushy about getting something more, thank goodness, so when he opened the car door for me and gestured for me to get inside, I smiled up at him.

"Thank you," I told him. And before he could reply, I closed the door behind him, and told the driver where I was headed. He might not have known it, but I was thanking him for reminding me just what it was like to have my mojo back after all this time. For reminding me that I could flirt with the best of them. And reminding me that, even if it hadn't been him, there were still men out there who wanted me, and who I could want right back.

It was amazing what just a little red lipstick could do for a girl, huh?

Chapter Three

Getting hot

"OKAY, I'M JUST NOT sure that it's really...me?"

"That's the whole point!" Natalia, the Polish hairdresser styling me, announced as she swiveled me around to look in the mirror. "You're totally new. Look! Don't you love it?"

I stared at myself in the mirror for a long moment and tried to come up with the words to react to what I saw in front of me. It wasn't just the hair, which I had paid Natalia to change – it was everything. Everything that I had put effort into over the last few weeks, it was finally starting to show, and I felt like I could see a whole new version of myself gazing back at my reflection in the mirror.

I had started off easy – purging my wardrobe and going around to the charity shops in town to see what I could find. I tried on pretty much everything all of them had in my size in the hopes of stumbling across something that worked for me, and I swear, I was on the point of becoming the first person ever to be outright banned from coming back to a charitable shop. I had dressed in my flowy clothes and long skirts for so long I had practically forgotten that there was anything else out there for me, but I managed to come across a few little bits and pieces that worked to change up what I already had without utterly changing the fundamentals of how I knew I felt comfortable. Some fitted jeans, some minimalist shirts that I had gotten tailored to hug around the actual shape of my body. Yeah, I was always going to be a hippy at heart, but that didn't mean that I could play dress-up as other characters too, did it?

My friend Emily had been more than happy to help out when I told her that I needed to update my make-up collection. Most of the products I owned, I had had since I was in high school, and I figured even for the sake of hygiene it was worth trying out something new. I didn't have much of a budget, but Emily was a make-up artist and knew all the cheap brands that secretly had great products. She let me pick her brain for hours, and even spent an afternoon showing me how to actually apply the stuff with some level of skill. Before that, I had known that contouring existed only as an abstract notion, but now I was nearly a dab hand at it myself.

And, of course, when I had finally let Mallory in on the truth of what I was doing, she had practically insisted that she set up an online dating profile for me.

"I don't know if I'm there yet..." I had protested, but she had waved her hand as she entered my details.

"If you're not there now, you're never going to be," she replied. "This way you can get to know them a little before you meet them, right? You won't just be heading out on dates at random."

"Not that I'm exactly doing that now," I pointed out.

"You're going to get out there and meet someone, I know it," she promised me, and I fought the urge to pull a face. I knew that she was just being positive, but I was still kind of nervous about the thought of getting out there into the world and just...and just *doing* the whole dating thing again. It had been so long since I had dared let myself stray there even inside my own head, not after what had happened with my ex...

"Hey, and no getting hung up thinking about what happened with the last guy you dated," she warned me, as though she could somehow see inside my head. I grinned at her. She was my best friend, after all – it was her job to get to know me inside and out. And it seemed like she had me totally figured out, whether I liked it or not.

"I'll try," I promised her.

"Now, what age range were you thinking for this next dude?" She asked. "Someone a little older? Younger?"

"I think someone older is what I'm looking for," I replied firmly. "I don't want to get involved with some kid, do I? Not if I actually want to settle down..."

"I guess so," She agreed. "So your age, maybe into their forties?"

"I'll let it down to thirty-five at the low end," I offered, hoping that it was going to be enough. "Just to widen my horizons."

"I'm not sure that your horizons are very widened with two more years, but alright," she agreed, giggling. "Man, this is fun. Do you think I should just forget about teaching and become a matchmaker?"

"See if you can make me a match first, and then we'll see," I replied, and she cocked her head, conceding the point.

"I'm sure I'm going to be able to do it," She told me. "You're a catch. You're going to be beating them back with a stick, trust me..."

"I'm not sure I have the energy for that," I groaned, and she punched me lightly on the arm.

"Come on, it's summer, you're starting over," she reminded me. "You've got energy for anything, don't you?"

"Within reason," I agreed, and she suddenly pointed her phone at my face.

"Okay, I need some pictures of you..."

"Why can't we just use the ones that I already have?" I protested, and she peered at me over the top of the phone for a moment.

"The ones that they took at the last school photo day?" She asked. "I'm not sure that puts forth the image you're trying to cultivate here..."

"Worth a shot, right?" I joked. "Maybe then they'd know that I'm serious about settling down..."

"Maybe so," she agreed. "But you're changing up your look. We want pictures that reflect that. Come on, smile..."

I posed for the pictures and tried not to feel too nervous about the way I looked now. I had to find some confidence, imbue it in the way that I moved through the world now. I wanted men to stop and stare at me. I knew it was a crazy thought, but maybe if I shot for the stars, I would land somewhere high in the sky, at least?

Mallory had consulted with me over the hairstyle that I was going to take on as part of this change, and we had settled on something simple and feminine and cute. I hadn't cut my hair in a long time – I guess it was something of a safety blanket, keeping it long and tawny and flowy, but it needed to go. Long hair was for princesses, and I was ready to graduate into my own royalty.

And, as I sat there and stared at myself in the mirror, I could hardly believe that I was actually looking back at myself. My make-up was crisp and nicely-applied – a casual, soft neutral eye, along with a subtle contour and even a little highlighter – and the shirt I was wearing drew this line from my chest to my waist that made me look way curvier than anything else I had in my wardrobe. My hair was feathered around my chin, hugging the loveheart shape of my face and trimmed to just below my shoulders. I was right; it wasn't me. But that was the whole point.

And suddenly, I found that I was looking back at the woman I had promised to find in amongst all of this. The woman who had confidence and wasn't afraid to strike out there into the world, to let everyone know that she was in charge and that nothing was going to change that. I had been pushing that woman down for a long time, but now she was here, and damn, I was *glad* for it. Because she looked good. And she had a smile on her face about half a mile wide as she took in the way she looked right now in the mirror.

"You like it?" Natalia asked proudly, as she saw the grin on my face. I nodded.

"I love it," I agreed. I paid her for her time and left a generous tip to thank her for her efforts, and I walked home along the River Ness feeling like my feet weren't quite touching the ground. It had been a long time since I had allowed myself to feel this way – to feel so bright and light and airy. I could feel the wind in my brand-new hair, and maybe it was just because I had had a few inches lopped off, but I was sure that I was carrying a little less weight right about now.

By the time I got back to my place, I was ready to enjoy some shameless enjoyment of my own reflection in the mirror in my bedroom. I pulled out the new clothes that I had purchased, held them up against myself, checked out how I could style this one, or this one, or this one, and I knew that I would be set for the next fifty dates that I went on.

If I got a single offer, of course.

No, I wasn't going to let myself think like that! I had spent long enough sitting on my rear end and feeling sorry for myself when it came to my romantic life, and I was totally done with it. It hadn't brought me any good – all it had brought me, in fact, was the need to completely revamp my entire life just to get back to anywhere that made sense.

But there was a reason for that. And, no matter how much Mallory might have wanted me to keep him out of my head, my ex was still very much present there right about now.

Lewis. I tried not to think about his name if I could avoid it. It wasn't that I missed him, exactly. No, in the time that we had spent apart, I had been able to see that he wasn't the nicest guy in the world – he could be impatient with me, and there was no doubt that he took his work as an accountant with more seriousness than he did anything else in his life. But we met at the right time, when the both of us were looking for the same thing at the same time, and it just made sense for me to be with him.

We had always been headed towards a family, the two of us, and I was sure that I was going to make one with him. He made good money, he was smart, and he was dedicated – he would make a good father, or at least, a good enough one. This had been five years ago, and even then, I had found myself worrying about the clock ticking down, about running out of time. Looking back now, I seemed so naïve - how could I think that it was even remotely a problem, given what I was dealing with right about now?

He had made me happy. Happy enough.

There was nothing wrong with him, and that was all I had needed at that point in my life, and so I committed to him. We had talked about marriage, and we had even started trying for kids – I was so excited, so excited at the thought of what was to come for us. Right up until the moment that I had been sitting in the doctor's office, of course, and she had told me that the tests had come back and that the chances of me having a baby through natural means was...

"Basically impossible," she had told me gently. And even though she had tried to be sweet about it, the memory of her voice in my head had come back to haunt me over and over and over again.

He hadn't been there with me at the appointment – he had seen no reason to be, and that had been that. But when I had come home and told him the truth about what the two of us were facing up to, I had known that it was the beginning of the end already.

He didn't say that was a reason why he had left me, but I knew for damn sure that it was. He didn't want to be with a woman who couldn't bear his children. He thought I was broken in some unfixable way – even though I had talked adoption and other options with him, he didn't seem to give a damn about any of them. His mind was made up, and he wanted someone who could give him what he truly wanted. And that person wasn't me.

I had moved out of the beautiful flat we had shared together, unable to afford anything close to the rent, and I supposed that I was in something like shock; when your whole life was ripped away from you like that, it was hard to feel anything other than total surprise. You build a future in your head, a life that you want to live out, and then it's snatched from you in an instant, and everything feels like it has come tumbling down around you in pieces. It was enough to put a girl off dating for life. Well, at least half a decade, in my case.

It was hard to believe that it had been five years since this had all started. I had taken all that time to try and get myself right again, all that space to convince myself that it was worth getting out there once more. It was hard to believe that there would be anyone out there for me, not after how he had treated me, not after he had dumped me because he knew I wouldn't be able to give him what he wanted. It felt like it had left a scar on me.

And it wasn't like other break-ups, where you could work on what had gone wrong and improve yourself from there on out. This would always plague me. Whoever I started dating next, I would have to sit there, at some point, and tell them the truth; that I couldn't have children, and if they wanted that from me, I couldn't do it the way they might want to.

That hurt. Even in the midst of all this change, I knew that I couldn't undo that. I couldn't find some way to fix it. I had to face up to it, one way or another. No matter how much I would have liked to pretend that none of it was happening, that none of it had happened.

I lay there on my bed and stared at the ceiling, and tried not to let the weight of what had crossed my mind weigh on me too much. There were a lot of men out there. A lot of men who might be more open to a different kind of lifestyle, a different kind of family. Now, I just had to focus my attention and energy on finding one who could handle everything that was going to come with dating me.

No matter how difficult it might have gotten.

Chapter Four

Fingers up your skirt

"I'M SURPRISED I NEVER came across you before," Announced Martin, the man sitting opposite me at this cramped table in this restaurant that looked as though it had recently been converted from a bomb shelter. I looked down at the glass of wine I had been sipping on, and sighed. I felt like I'd had this conversation a million times over already, and frankly, I was starting to get pretty sick of it.

Martin was the fifth man I had been on a date with this month, and I was starting to learn their scripts by heart. He was about my age, like the rest of them, and seemed to enjoy thinking of himself as the eternal bachelor type – or at least, he would have, if he could actually find women who were willing to date him.

And yet, here I was, sitting opposite him and listening to him talk and wondering how I had ended up on the same fucking date for what felt like the millionth time already. How could I be already getting tired of this? I was meant to be new to this scene, and yet it was starting to feel like I had been doing this for years.

On paper, Martin had looked pretty nice – handsome enough, bald and with a large beard, and he came from a rich family and seemed keen for me to know it. He had a good job – worked for the council – and he was smart enough to think that he could get away with being condescending to me. I should have taken that as the first warning sign that there was something off with him, but I had breezed forward anyway, convincing myself that I was just overthinking things and that I would have been better off just going along with it and not causing too much of a fuss. I had to meet people, didn't I, if I was going to date again, even if it meant people I wasn't totally certain about.

He had suggested a new Indian place for dinner, and I tried not to think about kissing someone with curry breath at the end of the night and got myself all dolled up and headed out to meet him. He looked a good ten years older than he had in the pictures on his profile, and he was even more condescending in person – he explained to me the meaning of the translations behind some of the dishes, and I just sat there and smiled along, knowing that rolling my eyes at him was just going to cause a bigger argument.

"Well, I only just started dating again," I offered him, hoping that everything I had seen of him so far was just bluster and that he actually had a good heart under all of that. It was something that came from years of teaching teenagers. A lot of them put on these big fronts only to cover up something deep and lonely underneath it all. But maybe I was being a little too kind, since this guy was hardly a teenager and he hardly had any excuse for the nonsense that he seemed insistent on pulling out here.

"I'm glad I found you so soon," he murmured, his voice dropping to what I supposed he believed was a sexy, sensual whisper. I had to press my lips together to keep from laughing out loud.

"I've actually had a few dates before this-"

"It's not going to be long until you're all used up," he continued, and my jaw nearly dropped. What the *fuck?* Was that what I had to look forward to now? This nasty attitude towards me, towards women in general...ugh. I winced, but before I could explain why, the waiter arrived to take our order and he loudly told him what we wanted to have. He stumbled over the pronunciation of some of the words and, tempting as it was to correct him, I decided it was best just to let it slide.

"So, what brings you back into dating?" He asked me, and I smiled and shrugged.

"I guess I'm just ready to find someone to settle down with," I replied, and he pulled a face.

"Can't think there's much good to settling down now," he remarked. "You must know how much fun there is to be had out there, right? You should go out and enjoy it. I know that's what I'm planning to do..."

Under the table, I felt his slithering fingers brushing over my bare knee. I didn't know whether he intended to do it or not, but nonetheless, I drew back from him at once. I had to repress a sigh of irritation. Great. Another guy who seemed to be after one thing and one thing only. That had been my problem with all of them so far, and frankly, I was getting tired of the boring innuendo and the assumption that I was looking for the same thing.

Nothing wrong with casual sex, but I had made it clear to all of these guys that I wanted something more. And they had just gone ahead and ignored that. No accounting for stupid, I guessed – even at this age, there were still some men who were thinking with their cocks first and foremost. Explained why they were all still single after all this time.

Though, in all fairness, one of them had actually forgotten to take off his wedding ring – he had tried to convince me that he was in the midst of a divorce, but I wasn't sure that I believed that for an instant. He looked way too shifty when he tried to feed me that line for me to come close to believing him. He was a bullshitter, and he was trying to drag me in along on his bullshit, and I had no room for that in my life, not one little bit. Not any longer, at least.

We ate our food, and it was only alright, and he talked a lot about how he knew good authentic Indian food and that this was it, through and through. I didn't have the heart to tell him that I had caught a glimpse of the packages they obviously heated up a lot of this stuff from in the kitchen when the door had swung open behind him. Maybe I should have – maybe that would have been enough to shut him up for a hot second, but I got the feeling that it wasn't going to be anywhere near that easy.

When we had finished dinner, he insisted on paying, despite my protests; I had learned the hard way that when men paid for dinner, they usually expected a different sort of payment in return, and that was one that I had no actual intention of giving to him. Not in a million years. Even though he had been nudging in that direction since the moment he had walked into this place and laid eyes on me.

"My place isn't far from here," he told me, leaning a little too close to murmur the words into my ear, to make sure that I really *got* what an amazing offer it was he was making me. Even if I had been looking for something casual, there was no way in hell I would have done it with him. Any guy that self-involved was going to carry that attitude right on over to the bedroom, and I was too much of an adult to put myself through the ritual humiliation of really bad sex these days.

"I think I'm just going to get a cab home," I told him firmly. His entire face dropped, like a kid who had just watched their scoop of ice-cream topple off the cone.

"But..." he tried to protest. I turned on my heel and swiftly walked away before he could make any further protests. *Nope, nope, nope.* I didn't want to have to handle this. I didn't want to deal with the baby-man-tantrum that I could tell he was on the brink of throwing. I knew it was coming, because I had already been forced to handle it a couple of times before this month, when I had apparently been giving off *signals* to the men I was with that had informed them that I wanted to go to bed with them.

Apparently, for guys this desperate, even the remotest amount of attention passed for signals, and I had figured out that the best way to get through to them was to be as blunt as I possibly could be.

No point getting their hopes up when I knew that nothing was going to come of this.

I made it back to my place before the sun was even down, and texted him to thank him for dinner but to let him know that I didn't think we were a good match for one another. I blocked his number after that; I had already had to deal with some level of wheedling from the guys I had shot down before, and frankly, I didn't have anything close to the energy to handle that right about now.

I took off my make-up and resented the effort I had put in to get ready when it had been a total bust. I should have just stayed at home, or called up Mallory and asked her to distract me for a while. I felt exhausted, and I had only been on five dates. But when all of them had been as rough as that, I felt like I couldn't be blamed for feeling pasted.

Five dates. Five dates, and I hadn't so much as kissed anyone yet. And damn, was there good reason for that; I could hardly imagine shaking hands with most of the guys I had met, let alone actually getting my face that close to theirs. Every time I found myself opposite one of them, I thought about whether I was reflected in this keen sense of desperation that I felt rolling off of them in waves. They might have been desperate for sex, while I was desperate for someone to settle down with, but maybe we weren't too far removed, after all. Maybe we weren't as far removed as I would have liked to think that we were.

Hopping in a quick shower before bed, I pulled the covers up to my chin and checked to see if I had received any more messages through the dating app while I had been out. Sure enough, there were a handful waiting for me. But I was too exhausted to think about replying to any of them. When I had started out on this a few weeks before, I had felt like I was riding high, reclaiming my mojo, coming back out and showing the world just what I could do. Now, I was considering joining a nunnery.

I slept in the next morning and texted Mallory to ask her to come out for a coffee with me; she agreed at once, and the two of us made it to our regular meeting spot, the Burgh, within a few minutes of one another.

"Well, well, well, if it isn't the most popular woman in the city," she teased as she joined me.

"Oh my God, I wish," I groaned. "I feel like I've been stuck on these shitty dates like it's Groundhog Day or something."

"So none of them have come to much?"

"None of them have come to anything," I sighed. "This guy last night, he made it pretty clear that he was just looking for someone to hook up with...."

"And did you?" She asked, leaning forward with interest.

"No!" I exclaimed defensively. "No, that's really not my thing, you know that. I don't...I want to know someone before I go there with them. And I didn't want to get to know this guy for anything, seriously."

"That's a shame," she sighed. "How many dates is that now?"

"Five," I replied, and I leaned my head on to my hands. I could hardly believe that I had made it to nearly a half-dozen dates without finding a single person who did anything for me. That felt like it had to go against some of the laws of nature, didn't it? Or maybe the dating scene in Inverness was much worse than I had ever imagined it to be.

"I think most of them want a younger woman," I explained. "Someone they can actually see starting a family with. Or else...or else it's just sex."

"Shit," she muttered, and she reached over to pat my hand. "You know it's going to be alright, yeah? We'll find you someone."

"But how?" I asked. "I feel like I've gone through most of the likely options for the guys I even remotely wanted to meet up with. I don't know who else is out there..."

"Yeah, but you're just talking about the guys that you've been with from your age group," she pointed out. I furrowed my brow at her.

"I really don't want to go a lot older than that..."

"Not older," she replied. "Younger. You could go a lot younger, couldn't you?"

"Oh, come on, I'm not looking to be someone's mother," I scoffed. I couldn't think of much worse in the world than having to attend to some twenty-something who was looking for someone to take care of his laundry as much as he was his dick.

"You don't have to go that young," she pointed out. "But maybe you could try...I don't know, just extending the age range by a few years. You could handle that, couldn't you? It could be fun. And I'm sure there are some guys out there who are looking for something more serious, even though they're a little younger. Just the same way there are guys our age who are still immature dicks even though they've got a few years on us."

"I suppose you have a point," I conceded reluctantly. I couldn't believe I was even letting myself think about this. Everything that had come through those dating apps had been a disaster so far, and I didn't see how any of that was going to change when it came to finding younger men.

"You remember those boys at the pub, right?" She reminded me. "They were younger than us, but they were nice."

"And you're still in touch with your one?" I asked playfully. She grinned at me.

"Hey, I told him that if he ever came through town again, he should hit me up," She replied. "That's the same thing, isn't it?"

"Close enough," I conceded, and she reached her hand towards me, palm up.

"What?"

"Give me your phone," she replied. "Let me change the age range for you. It won't take a second, but I don't trust you to do it yourself."

"I'm not totally tech-illiterate, you know," I pointed out, but I pulled my phone out and handed it to her.

"No, but you are a cynic, and I can see you being cynical about this," she replied, and she tapped in the code to my phone and went into the dating app. I knew that I could have protested and she would have stopped, but maybe she had a point; maybe I had to try opening myself up to something new. I felt like I had been doing so much of that lately that it was hard to imagine doing it and taking it any further than I already had, but I hadn't put all this effort in just to trip at the first hurdle and give up when things got a little tough. I had to keep going. No matter what. And if that meant fielding some messages from some guys in their late twenties looking to fulfill their older-woman thing, then so be it.

"Don't guys from that generation send pictures of their dicks to every girl they like?" I asked fretfully as she handed the phone back to me.

"Well, that's a quick way for you to weed out the ones who are obviously not worth it," she pointed out.

"I guess you have a point," I agreed, and I looked down a little fearfully at the logo that held the app. I supposed I was going to have to go a little out of my comfort zone to get what I wanted here. I certainly hadn't found it sticking with what I already knew, that was for sure. Maybe this was a good thing...?

Suddenly, a notification popped up on the app – I had a message. Already.

"Oh, someone messaged me!" I exclaimed, and Mallory clapped her hands together.

"Open it!" She ordered me. I hovered my thumb over the app for a moment, and then glanced at her.

"If this is a dick picture, then you owe me a slice of cake," I warned her. She held her hands up.

"That's a risk I'm willing to take."

I opened up the app, and clicked on the inbox to see what was waiting for me – and I burst out laughing when I caught a glimpse of it.

"What is it?" Mallory asked.

"You owe me a cake," I replied. "That's what."

Chapter Five

I want you

I FLOPPED DOWN ON the couch, picked up my glass of wine, and excitedly checked my messages to see if he had gotten back to me. There was nothing there, not yet, but I knew that he had his break in ten minutes, and when that came around he would be more than happy to chat me up again.

I took a sip of my wine and leaned back against the puffy cushion of my couch, and I couldn't keep the smile off my face a moment longer. I couldn't believe it. I had actually met someone. Someone who made me feel happy and buzzy and like I had something to look forward to when I was coming home at the end of a long day of teacher training. And we had never so much as met face-to-face.

This whole style of dating was utterly new to me, and I would have been lying if I said that I thought I had it in hand quite yet; it was difficult, not being able to see them in person, not being able to gauge our chemistry face-to-face. And yeah, there was something strange to me about being able to work on my dating life while I lay on the couch in a face mask working on a glass of wine. But maybe that was for the best. Maybe this was the future of dating. You got to know each other inside-out before you got to know anything else about them – how they looked, how they sounded, the way they laughed – and you had that to build on when you finally did meet.

When I had seen his name pop up on my phone, it had been like a flutter from my past had come back to haunt me. I had no idea where I knew that name from and I tried not to put too much thought into it, but he seemed familiar. Joseph Mackenzie. I winced when I saw how old he was – only twenty-eight, nearly ten whole years younger than I was – but his opening message was sweet and polite and curious and I figured that it was the least I could do to give him the time of day.

We exchanged a few messages at first, nothing deep or serious, but something about the way he spoke to me made me feel good about him. The other guys, they had been quick to forget their grammar, to communicate with emojis instead of actual words. It wasn't that I was totally averse to those things, but I felt like they were best used when you had already built a rapport with someone else. But he took his time, sending me these carefully thought-out messages that made me smile.

I would have met up with him already, but he worked offshore and was there for another couple of weeks before he made his return. I was already nervous about the thought of meeting him face-to-face.

What if he didn't like me? He had made it pretty clear that he thought I looked good in my pictures, but that was way different than actually laying eyes on me in person. Maybe he had misread my age. Maybe he thought I was younger. Maybe he had a fetish for older women and that was all that this was to him. Maybe, maybe, maybe...

"You need to stop worrying," Mallory had told me firmly when I had come to her with all of these concerns and worries running through my mind. I had forgotten, utterly and completely, how much this dating stuff could turn me into a total maniac. When I was single, I could convince myself that I was a pulled-together, intelligent woman with self-confidence and wit and the ability to tell when someone was leading me on and when someone actually liked me. When you put a man into the equation? Yeah, less so.

"I don't know if I can," I moaned, running my hand through my hair. I had been picking at the meal that we had ordered for lunch, my appetite lacking anyway, but I would have been lying if I'd said that there wasn't some part of me that was scared of gaining weight before I saw him again. What if he took one look at me and called me fat or something? Oh, there was no way in hell that I could handle that.

"Yes, you can," Mallory reminded me. "You were coping just fine without him in your life, weren't you? So it doesn't matter whether or not he stays in it, either way."

"I guess you have a point," I muttered, conceding to her. It was strange, though, even though I knew she was totally correct, there was some part of me that was already worried about the thought of losing him. Which was absurd, I knew that, given that I had only really had a relationship that had been conducted over text thus far, but it was the closest I'd had to anything that had made me feel truly alive in a long time. I didn't want to lose it.

"I know I do," She told me. "But still. You've actually met someone! I'm so excited for you."

"I think I'm excited too," I agreed, and she cocked her head at me.

"You only think you're excited?"

"I just don't know how I'm meant to feel!" I admitted, the words bursting out of me before I could stop them. "I was...I mean, I don't know if I was totally happy being single, but I was coping, that's for sure. Opening up to someone else like this...it's a lot to take in. It's more than I thought I would find so soon."

"You can always check out if it's getting to be too much for you," she reminded me gently. "You have the reins here, right?"

"Yeah, but I don't want to check out," I admitted. "That's what's freaking me out so much."

She reached across the table and squeezed my hand happily, a giant grin on her face.

"I knew we would find you someone," she told me proudly.

"Hey, we haven't even met in person yet," I protested. "I don't know if you should be getting so smug so soon."

"And yet, it's not going to stop me," she replied teasingly. "Come on, tell me some more about him. Let me live vicariously through you."

I started to fill her in on everything that had been happening in my life the last few days; even though we had been doing teacher training, we had been split off from each other given that we were both teaching different age groups, so we hadn't actually seen all that much of one another. And God only knew how much I needed her advice on all of this. I liked this guy so much, and yet I felt like I was so spectacularly useless when it came to dating that I had no actual clue where to start with getting him to fall for me.

"He's an engineer," I explained. "He works on the oil rigs off the North coast, he's been doing it for a while now. So he's not often back on the mainland..."

"Which means that you can totally take advantage of his enthusiasm when he is, right?" Mallory suggested, waggling her eyebrows at me pointedly. I gave her a look.

"Hey, I'm trying not to let that get into my head," I replied.

"But he is hot, right?" She asked. I grinned and looked down at my coffee. Truth was, he was so hot that when I had seen that he had messaged me, I had assumed that it had been some kind of mistake on his part – he couldn't possibly have bothered with someone like me, not when he must have had the whole pick of the women on that app at his fingertips.

He had short dark hair, the kind that waved slightly down around his ears, and these brown eyes that were flecked with gorgeous shimmers of gold. Even in his photographs, I could see how stunning they were, and I would have been lying if I'd said that I wasn't thinking about how sweet it would be to look into them in person. His work as an engineer had given him strong arms and a slim frame. He didn't look like those men that spent all their time down at the gym just to prove to themselves that they could lift this weight or that one; he looked like it came more organically, his muscles powerful and...mmm.

"Yeah, he's hot," I agreed. I would have shown her a picture, but for some reason I felt like that would have been jinxing it, and it was the last thing I wanted to deal with right now. This whole thing felt so precarious and I had no intention of doing anything that might send it spilling over the edge.

"I'm just worried that the age gap is going to be a problem," I admitted. "He must have so many girls after him, girls his own age, and I can't imagine that I'm going to be enough to keep his interest when they come calling..."

"Well, you've been enough so far, haven't you?" Mallory reminded me. "That's the thing about dating apps, you can choose from this wide range of people, so the ones you actually do reach out and message.. .well, you must really like them."

"I suppose so..."

"I mean, how many messages have you got from how many guys?" She pointed out. "And you're talking to him. I bet he's thinking just the same things that you are about you having better options."

"Or maybe he's hitting on me because he knows I don't have many," I replied nervously. I was just spouting off all my insecurities, and I knew they sounded crazy coming out of my mouth, but I needed to have someone there to stand by and tell me that I was okay, that this was going to be fine. It didn't help that I had yet to see him in person. I could have put this to the back of my mind had we actually spent some time together, had we actually felt the chemistry that I was so sure that we shared.

"You need to start treating yourself with a little more kindness," she warned me. "You're my best friend, and I'm afraid I won't stand for people being mean to you, alright? You've found someone. He likes you. He's not doing this for any reason other than that."

"You sure you're not paying him off?" I asked, half-joking.

"What do I look like, I'm made of money?" She replied. "Even if I could, I wouldn't have to. You're a catch, Abigail, you need to stop being so hard on yourself."

"I'll try," I promised her, and I supposed that I meant it. I needed to start believing that I was actually worth this man's attention, even though I couldn't figure out why he was so interested in me.

He liked me. He liked me a lot.

And I liked him a lot right on back.

We talked about books and movies, where we'd grown up – it turned out that he lived not far from the school I taught at, and we shared a few favorite memories of the place. He was smart and eloquent and seemed to actually want to put in the time to get to know me, and he was good at keeping up a conversation. So many of the guys on this app just seemed to hit a wall at a certain point and would run out of things to say to me, offering up nothing but useless platitudes. I didn't have that problem with Joseph. He was curious to know every detail of my life, and I was flattered that he seemed to have such an interest in me.

It was that evening, about two weeks after we had started talking, that he dropped the bombshell – he wanted to meet with me.

"I'm going to be back on shore at the end of next week," He explained. "I was hoping that I might be able to take you out for dinner. Or drinks. Or maybe both."

I smiled when I looked at the message and tried to quell the swell of nerves that came as soon as I took in what he was saying. I could play at being this cool, clever version of myself over messages, but I had no idea if I was going to be able to make that work when I actually saw him in person. Would I just be stumbling over my words, useless, making a fool of myself?

I could hear Mallory's voice in my head, telling me to get on with it and to tell him that I wanted to meet him and that I would just love the chance to spend some time with him out in the real world, but my fingers seemed to have turned to lead and I had no idea how to express any of that to him at that moment. I dumped my phone on the table, and instead sat there, working on my glass of wine.

I should have just pulled myself together and said yes to him. I liked talking to him, and I was attracted to him, and I was sure that those things were only going to become more true once I actually saw him in person, but still, I was having trouble telling myself that this was the right choice. There was a part of me, I supposed, a not-so-small part of me, that was worried that I was leading him on. I couldn't have kids, I couldn't have a family of my own, shouldn't I have come out and told him that? Or would that have been way too much way too soon? I wished someone could just hand me a set of rules that I could use so that I wouldn't make a total ass of myself around him.

As I worked my way through the glass of wine, I started wondering – was this how it was always going to feel when I was around new people? When I met new guys? Would I always have that doubt in my mind, the fear that I wasn't enough for them, and that they should have been allowed to know that sooner rather than later? The scars my ex had left on me were still just as powerful as they had ever been, and I hated myself for letting my mind give in to them. I couldn't keep living in the past. I had to look forward. It was time to accept that I had a future in front of me, and that I wasn't willing to hold back on it any further.

I grabbed my phone and looked at his message again. Suddenly, I felt a little rush of excitement run down my spine. It felt like sparkles, lighting up my whole body, and I couldn't help but smile. It had been a long time since I had allowed myself to feel that about anyone – for the most part, accepting real sweetness, real romance into my life had only brought struggle, the reminder of what I was unable to do. But this seemed different. Maybe I was just being naïve, maybe I was crazy for believing that things would be different this time around, but I did. I wanted to. I was ready, God knew how ready, just to let go of everything I had been holding back on all this time and let myself have a little fun for a change.

It seemed like it took me about a straight half-hour to put together a message that I actually wanted to send him. How to sound interested, but not so interested that it came off as desperation? I didn't like the idea of putting him off with my keenness, but I didn't want him to think that I was just doing this out of boredom, out of lack of a better option presenting itself. Because that *so* wasn't the case.

Finally, I felt like I had landed on something I could be happy with. I looked it over again, and bit my lip – now, I just had to send it to him. I wondered if he was out there, surrounded by the slightly peeling walls of the break room that he had sent me pictures of the day before, staring at his phone, waiting for my message, waiting to hear from me again after all this time. I liked the thought of that. I knew it was a little self-involved, but I wanted him to be thinking about me. I wanted him wondering about my state of mind, what I was doing, what I was thinking, whether I felt the same way about him that he did about me.

Well, I did. And I had no intention of playing hard to get a moment longer. Taking a deep breath, I sent the text – just a casual, *sure, I'd love to, where were you thinking?* - and watched as it zoomed off into the annals of the metaverse, to be carried across the sea towards him. I watched the screen for a moment or two longer, waiting for the blip that would tell me that it had reached him alright, and sure enough, there it was.

I clasped my phone to my chest and closed my eyes. Yes, I was nervous. Yes, I was already freaking out about this. And yes, I was already wondering if I hadn't just somehow managed to send the stupidest text in all of recorded history and not have noticed it. But for now, I had something to look forward to. I had a date on the way. And not one part of me could wait.

Chapter Six

Let me worship your body

I STARED AT MY nails. Should I have picked a different color?

I had gone for dark blue, but maybe I should have shot for something more girly – a pale pink, perhaps? No, I was too old for that these days. Perhaps a vampy red? Ugh, like I could actually pull off anything that was meant to be sexy...

I clasped my hands in my lap and drew my attention away from them. I needed to calm all the way down and relax. This was what dating again did to me, apparently, got me shooting off in a million different directions about all the choices that I should have made differently before I came out here to meet Joseph for the first time.

Checking my watch for the fiftieth time since I had arrived, I chewed on my lip. I had left the house early, since I had never been to this bar that he had suggested before and I didn't want to turn up late, but as it transpired, I was there fifteen minutes early. Maybe that would come across as too keen? I couldn't tell.

It doesn't matter, I tried to soothe myself. *You are keen. No need to hide from that.*

I didn't believe it.

The bar he had chosen for us couldn't have been more perfect; I was surprised that I had never come across it before in all the time I had spent in Inverness. It was set on the ground floor of the hotel that stood next to the train station, and the whole place was cloaked out in gorgeous reds and golds, the chairs upholstered with a haughty clan tartan, and stuffed stag heads mounted on every wall. It was quiet, but not so quiet that I had to worry about some exposé in the Courier about rats in the kitchen or something. Just a little hidden gem, a part of the city that I had never known about before I'd met him. I had to admit, he was already doing pretty well.

Mallory had helped me pick out an outfit for the night, and I liked what I was wearing – despite my silly panic over my nails. It was a short black dress that flicked out around the thighs and showed off a little leg, but not too much. I wanted to look like I at least had a little self-respect to hang on to, even though I had understood the term *panty-dropper* as soon as I had seen him for the very first time.

God, I was excited.

He had messaged me earlier in the day to let me know how much he was looking forward to our time together, but I doubted that this was his first date in years, like it was for me. I was back on the scene at last, and with a bang, too - or at least a pop. He was gorgeous, smart, attentive, gorgeous... though I think I mentioned that one already. I hoped that he was as attractive in person as he was in–

And before I could think another word, he walked in. And the whole world stopped moving for a moment.

No wonder they had to keep him all the way out there on the oil rig for most of the year – if he had been on land year-round, he would have caused riots. He was tall, a solid six feet, with that dark, curly hair a little grown out and a smattering of deep brown stubble over his chin. His brown eyes scanned the room for a moment, and it was like the breath had been knocked out of my body. How was I meant to think straight when he was right there, looking like...looking like *that?*

Finally, his eyes landed on mine, and a huge smile cracked out over his face. I smiled back, and I rose to my feet as he got closer to me.

"Abigail," he greeted me with my full name; his voice was deep and rich, a little gruff around the edges, just the way I had imagined it. Not that I, of course, had spent any time at all imagining it.

"Joseph," I breathed back, and he ducked in to give me a kiss on the cheek in greeting. Mmm – his aftershave was something expensive, something classic and masculine and spicy, though there was something else going on underneath it that had my hair standing on end. I wanted to bury my face into his neck, but I figured that might have been a little forward.

When he pulled back, I felt like my feet were barely touching the ground. Could he feel it, too? The way he was smiling at me, he had to be able to feel it – to feel the rich, powerful lust between us, that seemed to block out everything in the room. He was wearing a button-down shirt in a soft, pale blue, and I wanted nothing more than to send all the buttons scattering to the floor around us.

"Can I get you something to drink?" He offered, gesturing to the bar.

"I would love that," I agreed, deciding to stick to short sentences for now. Best to make sure that I didn't come across like a totally monotonous fool.

"Red wine, right?" He asked, and I nodded and smiled. I couldn't remember mentioning it to him, but in the flurry of messages that we had explained, it was natural that I would have forgotten something.

"You grab a seat. I'll get us our drinks," he told me, and I did as I was told. When he spoke, it was like something deep and profound within me just wanted to obey. I wouldn't have described myself as a naturally rebellious person, but I couldn't think of a time when someone had managed to have this profound of an effect on me within moments of us first meeting one another.

He headed back with our drinks a moment later. When he sank down into the thickly-padded armchair next to mine, I found myself gazing at him stupidly. I knew that I shouldn't have been so damn obvious, but it was so hard not to stare when everything about him was just so perfect.

"Feels a little odd to be here in person, right?" He remarked, and I nodded, glad that he had given me a cover for the way that I was ogling him.

"Yeah, little odd," I echoed, and I took a sip of my wine. It tasted expensive. I liked it at once, and allowed it to seep into my system and get me feeling a little less nervous about how this was going to go.

"It's so good to meet you properly," he murmured to me, and his eyes scanned back and forth over my face as he took me in. "I thought about you a lot out there. Feels like I've known you forever."

"Yeah, I know what you mean," I agreed.

There was something profoundly familiar about him, something I hadn't yet been able to put my finger on. I put it down to some deep soul connection, perhaps.

That was easier to explain than anything else.

From there, the conversation started and didn't stop for another two whole rounds; he was as eloquent and charming as he had been over the phone, and I adored his company more than I could find words to say. I noticed that a few women glanced in his direction when they saw me with him, and I found myself feeling that little zing of triumph knowing that I was the one he had chosen to be with for the course of the night. I felt like showing off, telling the world that he had picked me and that they should be jealous.

He told me about his life out on the rig, the assholes he had to work with, the friends he had made as part of the company. Sharp, witty, and bright, his words kept me engaged all night long until the light had begun to dim in the city streets beyond the windows, and a little rain had started to patter up against the glass. The sound of it was soft, soothing, much like the sound of his voice as it slipped through me. I felt like I could have listened to him speak all night long.

He was curious about my life, as well, though he didn't pry; he let me set the tone for what I wanted to tell him, and I found myself spilling more than I thought I would have the nerve to. He made me feel so comfortable in just telling him all this stuff that I would have kept wrapped up and quiet before, all these secrets that I knew I should have kept to myself. Like who I had dated in high school, where I lived, how long I had stayed there alone, the dreams I had about moving out to the Orkney islands and teaching there...it wasn't anything scandalous, but I shouldn't have been dropping so much of it on his lap out of nowhere. I was meant to be holding back, wasn't I? Playing it at least a little *somewhat* cool. But I felt like I had been holding back long enough in the time that I had known him, and now that he was here before me, I had no intention of doing it for a moment longer.

"I've traveled up to the islands a few times," he remarked. "It's gorgeous out there. When you can see it through the mist, I mean."

"You should take me next time you go," I told him, and I realized at once how those words must have sounded coming out of my mouth – talk about being a little forward on a first date.

"Oh, I didn't mean it like..." I began to correct myself, but before I could finish up, he had reached out and covered my hand with his. He was smiling at me. I had thought he would run for the hills as soon as I gave him a hint of what was actually going on inside my head, but if anything, he seemed to like it.

"I would love to take you there one day," He replied, and he squeezed my hand softly. The pressure of his skin next to mine made my heart sing for a split second. My breath caught in my throat, and I had to calm myself before steam started coming out of my ears. His thumb grazed over my knuckle, leaving a hot trail right behind it as it went. I could already feel a heat beginning to build between my legs. I needed him. I knew that it was too soon, but I needed him, and I couldn't imagine holding back even if it was a really bad idea. I was certain there were rules for this kind of thing, rules that would have told me that the best thing I could do was hold back and leave him wanting more, but there was no way I could let that happen when all I needed was...

"Do you want to walk me home?" I asked him, suddenly. We were halfway through our drinks so there would have been no reason for us to leave, but the thought of being stuck here and surrounded by all these people when the only thing I wanted was to get my hands all over him made my chest hurt.

"Right now?" He asked, sounding surprised. I nodded.

"Right now," I agreed. My heart was pounding and I was sure that he was going to politely turn me down, maybe let me know that he liked me so much as a person but that this wasn't going to work out. I didn't know that I could have handled it if he had. I mean, I would have found a way, of course, but when I looked at him it seemed as though everything just made sense and clicked into place. I needed more of him.

"Of course," he replied at once, and he threw back the last of the whisky in his glass and got to his feet. Offering me a hand, he pulled me up to stand beside him, and for a split second, it took everything that I had in me not to lean up and kiss him. God, if I could have just let it happen...my body ached for it, my lips suddenly parched for his touch. Did he know what he was doing to me? Did he know how long it had been since I had felt like this for anyone? Did he know that I was beginning to wonder if I had ever really felt like this before in my life?

He held on to my hand as we made our way out of the bar, and I noticed the barmaid giving us a knowing look – I was sure she knew just what was going to happen as soon as we were out of there, but I found it hard to give a damn about being the subject of her idle glance.

Outside, the rain had started to ease off, but he still offered me his jacket. He was such a gentleman. But, in truth, I wanted to take it off him myself when the time was right. Like I was unwrapping a gift I had been waiting for as long as I could remember.

"So, where is it you live?" He asked. I tugged him forward, amazed at how well our hands seemed to fit together.

"I'm always better at showing over telling," I replied, and he laughed and followed behind me. I didn't mind that it was cool that night for summer, and I didn't mind that the streets were quiet and that our voices echoed around to fill them; I only cared that he was here, that he was finally, truly here, and that I could finally, truly call him my own. The way he was looking at me made my belly feel like it was burning. The water of life, that was what they called whisky, and that was what I was looking forward to tasting on his lips as soon as I got the chance.

I needed to know how it felt to kiss him, more than I had needed to know that about anyone before in my life.

I could almost imagine the way that he would get me to yield to his touch...

Finally, we arrived outside my block of flats, and I looked up at him. This was where I had to find the nerve to tell him that I wanted him to come upstairs with me. Had I ever done this before? I had normally let the men take the lead, but, as he looked down at me, I knew I would need to strike out first this time around. He was too much of a gentleman to push any further than he already had, and I wanted him to know that he was more than welcome to do anything he wanted to me now that he was finally there in front of me.

"I don't usually do stuff like this," I blurted out, instantly cursing myself for sounding like such a dork. "But...but do you want to come inside?"

Without bothering to speak his reply, Joseph slipped his hands either side of my cheeks, and gazed down at me. God, my heart was beating so hard right then, I could hardly keep a handle on it. I wanted him to kiss me, but at the same time, I wanted to hang out in this moment forever. I saw his gaze drift down to my lips, and I knew that he was savoring in this the same way I was, letting himself get lost to me.

"You have no idea how long I've waited for this," he breathed. And with that, he finally sealed his lips over my own.

As soon as our mouths met, any last doubts that I might have been having over whether or not this was a good idea slipped out of my head for good. Nothing mattered. Nothing mattered anymore, because I finally had him, finally had the man that I had been thinking about for so long.

He parted my lips with his tongue and drew me against him passionately, letting out a moan that seemed to rush through my whole body at once. Every nerve-ending was lighting up. Had I always had this many? It felt like new ones had manifested as he kissed me for the first time, as though my body was having to change the very way that it was built so it could make sense of the way his body felt against mine.

He wrapped his arms around me tight and pulled me close. I could feel my body shaking slightly, and it had nothing to do with the weather. I had dreamed that this night would end this way, of course I had, but I had never in a million years actually believed that I would end up here. I didn't think I would have the nerve. I didn't think we would have the chemistry. But here we were, kissing in the street, like we couldn't wait a moment longer.

When he pulled back, there was a soft smile on his face. I smiled back at him.

"I think I want to come inside now," he told me, and though he was leaving that choice to me, I knew that it was more an order than anything else. An order that I was more than willing to give in to.

I kissed him again, not able to speak with words everything that I was feeling, and I unlocked the door and led him up the stairs towards my home. It felt almost a little surreal to have him here, after so long dreaming about it. In some ways, it felt like it wasn't the first time that he had walked into my home; it felt like he had belonged here all along. I had spent so many hours on that couch, thinking about him, thinking about how sweet it would be to be with him in that moment, it was almost like he had been there before.

I pulled him over the threshold to my bedroom, my hands on his sides, and his teeth caught on my lip – it was just for the briefest moment, the sharpest feeling of shock and pain that made me shiver. But then, he kissed me better, and I kissed him back again, and the only thing my body seemed to be built for right then was his.

He pushed me down onto the bed, and he slipped his hands up my sides so that he could pin my arms above my head. I parted my lips and let out a moan, and he buried his face into my neck. I could feel his stubble catching on my skin but I didn't mind it, not one bit. This was what I had wanted from the moment I had seen him. I was shocked that I had been able to hold myself back for so long. His body felt so good pressing down on top of mine, the weight of it comforting, in some strange way. Like a reminder that he was more than powerful enough to keep me safe if the time ever came to call for it.

He smelled even better close up, with the scent of my skin mingling with his. I could already feel his hardness, even through his jeans, the tangle of our legs drawing us closer and closer together. I wanted to feel him inside of me. It was the first time I had felt a need that had taken control of me this much; I had had sex before, of course, but it had mostly been to please the men I was with, not because I felt that deep, abiding want myself. But now? Now, it was all coming from me. And I wasn't willing to slow down.

I reached down and grabbed his ass, pulling him greedily towards me. God, he felt good. I couldn't wait to feel him fill me up. I wanted to tell him that we could go raw and that there was nothing to worry about, but I figured that it wasn't quite time to come out about all of that yet. I could hold back, I could wait.

He was kissing down my neck and towards my chest, and I felt this little jolt of nerves as he got down there; what if he stripped me down and I wasn't what he had expected? I knew that the chances of that happening were tiny, but I couldn't help but feel a little nervous despite that. He had probably been with any number of gorgeous women in his time; look at him, I was sure that he had. I just hoped that he wasn't going to be disappointed by the way I looked.

He slipped his fingers beneath the straps of my dress and eased down my arms; I had to fight the urge to, on instinct, cover myself up. Me and my ex, we had mostly done this stuff in the dark, and I was quite sure that it had a lot to do with the fact that he didn't care much for my body. He had left me with a complex, and I was so freaked out that I was going to let Joseph down, too – or that he would sense my insecurity, and that would be enough to...

And then, he lowered his mouth to my nipple, and everything slipped out of my head for a moment.

The warmth of his breath on my skin felt, for a split second, like more than I could take; I had to catch my breath, reaching down to trace my fingers through his hair and feel the heat of his body on top of mine. He moaned softly, and the feel of the vibration passing through my body made everything squirm to life. He bared his teeth, letting them catch against my breast, and I gasped and wriggled beneath him. I couldn't stop myself. I didn't want to. I just wanted this, this, this, him, him, him, and I had been waiting far too long for it to happen in the first place. What had I been so worried about? He looked up at me, flicking his gaze to meet mine, and I leaned down to kiss him. I couldn't resist.

I needed to feel his naked body, that I was sure of. I had never felt a craving so sharp and so sure in my life before. I reached for the buttons of his shirt, my fingers shaking slightly, and I began to undress him; God, I wanted him. I could already feel the slickness inching its way down my thighs. This dress seemed to be getting in the way more than anything else, our clothes nothing but a distraction from the main event.

"Here, miss," he murmured, brushing my hands away and taking over. "Let me."

I watched him as he stripped down, my heart palpitating hard in my chest as I waited to see him; I had tried to picture what his body would have looked like so many times before, but I doubted even in my wildest dreams I would have been able to come up with something as intensely beautiful as this.

He was strong and powerful, and when he moved, I could see his muscles snaking beneath his skin like they were struggling to stay contained; I reached up to run my hand over his chest, marveling at the feel of his strength beneath my fingers. I noticed that his chest was rising and falling swiftly, and realized that I was making him wait for something that I was all too keen to start on myself.

Pulling me upright, he didn't waste any time in stripping me down so that he could have me naked; I hadn't bothered with a bra, and all that I had left on when he disposed of the dress were a pair of panties. He leaned back on the bed, taking me in, checking me out, as I squirmed with delicious anticipation in front of him.

"God," he murmured, and he ran his hands up my legs. "You're so fucking perfect..."

And with that, he pushed my thighs apart, and he slipped down between them. Planting his mouth against my pussy through my panties, he drew a loud moan from between my lips; before, I had made noise in bed basically to encourage the guys that I was with that they were doing a fine job, but with him, it felt different. It felt like I couldn't have kept it in even if I had wanted to. He slipped his fingers around the hips of my panties and eased them down my legs, moving so that he could toss them aside and have me utterly bare beneath him.

"Can I go down on you?" He asked, his voice low with a hungry desire, as he brushed his fingers over the puff of hair on my mound. I nodded.

"Please," I murmured back, and with that, he dived between my legs, and tasted me for the first time.

"Fuck," I groaned, and I found my fingers closing around the sheets on the bed as I tried to make sense of the pleasure that he sent coursing through me at once. It wasn't like this was the first time that I'd ever had a guy go down on me, but this was...this was different. This wasn't like any of the other guys who had taken a trip South before; they had all seemed like they were doing it because they felt they had to, or just to get the same from me. But when Joseph did it, it felt like he honestly couldn't get enough of me.

He sealed his lips around my clit to start, stroking me from side to side with his tongue and letting out a long growl of pleasure that seemed to course through every inch of my body. His mouth was warm and soft and eager and I could feel the roughness of his stubble against my skin; fuck, he was so *good.* His lips traced every part of me, exploring every inch of me that he could, and I lay my head back and just let the pleasure take control of me.

I might have felt selfish, before, about just letting him pleasure me while I did nothing in return. But there was no room for cogent thought when he was between my legs and treating me this way; everything slipped out of my head, leaving a welcome quiet that I didn't often find inside my brain.

He took hold of my hips to keep me in place and he went down on me like his life depended on it. And I lay there and let him – let me lavish me with attention from his tongue, let him do whatever he wanted to me. He let his tongue trace down to my slit for a moment, before he swirled it in soft, quick circles around my clit, and I swear it was like the whole room was spinning around me. It had nothing to do with the alcohol, and everything to do with him, him, him...

I started getting close, the fire on my belly growing and building until I couldn't hold it back any longer. I reached down to grab hold of his shoulders, feeling that muscle beneath my fingers, letting them trace the shapes of his body as I half-crunched up off the bed. When I came, a sound close to a wail burst out of my lungs, and I felt the pleasure flood through me like a dam had burst to fill me from the crown to the toes full of lust, of want, of need.

Pulling him on top of me, I kissed him again, frantic for more. I could taste myself on his lips, and it only made me hungrier for him.

"Fuck me," I pleaded, and I reached into the bedside table to grab a condom for him. I pushed it into his hand, and helped him as he undressed from the waist down – and as soon as I laid eyes on his cock, my jaw nearly dropped.

He was perfect. Long, thick, gorgeous – God, if I hadn't been so keen to feel him inside of me, I would have been begging to take that thing into my mouth instead. I watched as he sheathed himself, and I scooched down the bed a little and spread my legs beneath him.

"Please," I moaned, and I watched as he slowly guided himself towards my soaked pussy.

He groaned as he lowered himself into me for the first time, as though this was what he had been waiting for as long as he could remember. I knew just how he felt. I might not have been able to put it into words when I had first seen him, but I had been dreaming of this right from the moment I had set eyes on him, on the blurry screen of my slightly crappy phone. I had felt that chemistry then, that connection, undeniable. Not that I would have wanted to deny it, not for a moment...

He took me slowly at first, letting me get used to the feeling of him moving inside of me, and I was grateful for his patience; it had been a long time since I'd had anyone else in my bed like this, and it took a moment for my body to remember exactly how to accommodate him. Not to mention the fact that he was so damn *big* too.

But soon enough, I had grown used to the feeling of him inside me. More than used to it. As he moved into me in long, slow strokes, I could feel an addiction growing all at once, an addiction that I was going to have a hard time stemming. Even the thought of this being over made me feel unhappy; but I forced myself to kiss him again, and to just live in the moment, to give myself to the way that he made me feel.

I wrapped my legs around him and arched my back so that I could push against him harder and with more purpose; I wanted him as deep inside of me as I could manage. I wanted his body as part of mine. His mouth was on my neck, his stubble grazing at my skin, and I cupped the back of his head in my hand and held him there, held him close, telling him without words that I didn't want him to go anywhere and that as long as I had a choice he would be here, right here, with me.

It wasn't long before I could feel the orgasm building again. It stirred deep down inside of me, the pleasure reaching almost unbearable levels before I felt it crest and break once more; fuck, it felt incredible, the magic of my body and his and the way they came together like they had been built for one another a gift that I was never going to get over. I kissed him as I came, breathed my pleasure into his mouth, and felt like I could have lost myself in that moment for the rest of time and been happy with it.

As my pussy clenched around his cock, I felt him cum, his dick twitching as he spilled his seed inside of me. I let my teeth catch on his lip and I felt his entire body shudder, whether from the pleasure or the pain, I couldn't tell.

He pulled back and looked at me and it was as though he was marveling at how perfect I was. I looked right back at him, feeling the exact same way.

I couldn't believe that this man, this gorgeous, perfect man, I couldn't believe that he actually wanted me. And there was no way he was faking it. He couldn't have conjured up the passion that he had addressed me with before; he couldn't have invented it.

He was really into me.

He kissed me again as he slowly slipped out of me, and then slid down beside me, sprawled out on my bed. He extended an arm so that I could snuggle into him, and I did as he offered at once. He smelled so good, maybe because the scent of the two of us had begun to mingle on his skin. I buried my face in his chest and listened to the calming *thud thud thud* of his heart.

And, even though I knew that I should have kicked him out, that it was way too early for me to be even thinking about letting him stay the night, I felt my eyes drifting shut.

Maybe just this once, I could do it and get away with it.

Wasn't this all about changing up the way I had done things before, after all?

The old version of me, she might have shied away from doing something like, from diving in so fast and so soon. But this new version? Yeah, she was going to fall asleep right here, and she wasn't going to beat herself up about it.

And she was going to enjoy waking up next to this perfect man the next morning.

Chapter Seven

Get out of my house

When I came to the next morning, it took me a moment to remember what had happened the night before.

I could remember going to that little bar near the station, I could remember putting away a fair few drinks there. I could remember meeting Joseph, and I could remember looking at him and thinking *woah.* I could remember asking him to walk me home, and I could remember him agreeing...

Oh.

And then the rest of it all started coming back to me, too. The rest of the memories that we had made last night. It took me a moment to slot them all into place, but as soon as I did, I squirmed against my sheets and smiled at the ceiling. That had been *good.* Seriously good.

I glanced over beside me, and sure enough, there he was fast asleep next to me. He looked a little younger than he had last night now that he was asleep, all the muscles in his face relaxed. I reached over and traced my fingers over his cheek; his skin was so soft. I would need to get him to drop a skincare routine. I stifled a giggle at the thought, and he rolled over, and wrapped his arms around me, pulling me tight against him. I closed my eyes and let him, snuggling back against him happily. I was about to let myself drift back off to sleep...when all the insecurity that I had tried to shut out last night came flooding back into my head once more.

I couldn't believe I had allowed him to stay the night here. I couldn't believe that I had let him...well, that we had hooked up so soon after we had first met in person. And if I was being honest with myself, I had been the one behind all of that. He had given me all the power, asked me what I wanted, and I had told him to keep going. Fuck, I don't think that I could have asked him to stop even if I'd wanted to; when he touched me, when he laid hands on me like that, I felt like I was utterly helpless before him. I wondered if I made it obvious. He just drove me crazy, he had done from the moment I had laid eyes on him in that damn bar...

I wriggled out from under his grasp and slipped over to the edge of the bed. I needed to clean myself up. When he woke up, I didn't want him to see the smeared make-up from last night on my face. Did I just go with a bare face, or did I try to reapply and hope that he wouldn't notice that I had a full face of make-up on first thing in the morning? I was a little nervous about the thought of being blatant and honest with him, especially when he had only seen me in full date mode the night before.

I tried to calm myself down. I was freaking out over nothing. Nothing! I knew I didn't have anything to worry about, not really, and yet I was bending over backwards to convince myself that he would have been just *disgusted* if he'd gotten a look at me first thing in the morning. I had had the same panic the night before, when he had been undressing me, but I supposed the sheer animal need that I had for him had been enough to get me over the worst of that. Now, though, now it was the clear light of morning, and I had to accept the fact that I was more than ten years older than this man and that it was going to be harder to hide that now that the sun was out once more...

This was exactly why I had promised myself that I wasn't going to bring him home. Say that all he was after was casual sex? Well, he'd gotten it now, and there would be no reason for him to come back for more. Was he one of those guys who just ticked girls off his list and that was that? Maybe he didn't even work offshore. Maybe that was just something he told the hapless women he hooked up with to keep them off his back and make sure that he didn't have to bother getting too committed.

I showered and made myself a coffee, and glanced in on him as I went; still asleep. So at least he wasn't going to be able to make a break for it while I was looking away. Was that still a thing that people did? Left in the middle of the night to avoid waking up the person they had been sharing a bed with? I had been out of the game for so long that I could honestly say that I had no real idea.

I needed to call Mallory. She would know what to do. Even if that was just telling me that I was freaking out about nothing and that I needed to calm the hell down and stop panicking about what was going on. In fact, I could just about synthesize the advice that she would give me inside my own head. *You're a grown woman. You can have sex with who you want. Who cares if you liked each other that much right away? You've been talking for weeks now anyway...*

And that was about enough to make it sting a little less. I didn't need to worry about this. Did I? I mean, yes, in a perfect world, maybe I wouldn't have gone home with him so soon. But I liked him. I really liked him. And I was seriously attracted to him. Besides, it wouldn't be long until he had to ship off again, and there was no part of me that was willing to wait so long for him to come back. I would have blown a fuse if I'd had to wait that much longer.

At the very worst, even if he never called me again, I could put this little escapade down to me juicing up my mojo a little, reminding myself that I was still a sexy woman with sexy-woman-needs. If I could get a guy like that into bed, I couldn't imagine that I would doubt myself when it came to anyone else.

I sipped on my coffee, and when I was finished, I scrubbed my teeth to make sure that I didn't have nasty breath when he came to. I didn't want to scare him off for anything. Last night had been so damn good, I hated the thought of missing out on another round of it.

Deciding to slip back through to join him in the bedroom, I perched on the edge of the bed and watched him rest a little longer; he didn't snore, just breathed deeply, like he was trying to inhale everything in the room around him. I was about to snuggle down in bed next to him again – and hopefully wake him up for another round of fun when he felt up to it – something caught my attention from the corner of my eye.

I looked over, and saw his phone on the bedside table. It had lit up, letting him know that he had a message. But that wasn't what made my heart drop with panic.

The picture on his phone was of him, with a couple of women – well, one woman, and a girl, really. I reached out for his phone with trembling fingers, and slowly picked it up. There was no way that I could be seeing what I thought I was. There was just no *way*...

I knew the girl in the picture, the one that he had his arm slung around in a way that spoke to his familial familiarity with her. She had dark hair, the same eyes as him, and her name was Mary Mackenzie.

And she went to my school.

That alone would have been strange enough to raise some serious questions, but it was all the pieces I put together afterwards that really made my stomach turn. If it had just been her, then that would have been one thing; it would have been odd, and I would have asked him about it, and I was sure that he would have come up with a decent excuse to palm me off and convince me that he had done nothing wrong.

But I had finally figured out where I knew him from. He had gone to the school I taught at, too. I had never been one of his teachers, thank goodness, but he had only left about six years ago, which meant that he couldn't be older than twenty-four.

I had a sudden flashback to our encounter the night before, when he had called me *miss* in bed, and I felt a panicked shiver run down my spine. Oh, no. Oh, *no.* That meant that he had to know, right? That he had deliberately decided not to tell me?

Oh my God. I tossed the phone back on the bedside table, where he had left it. I had sat opposite his mother at parent-teacher nights, for goodness sake. She was on the PTA. And I had just fucked her son. I had just hooked up with him. And it had been some of the best damn sex of my life.

The sound of the phone clattering down on the bedside table was enough to stir him from his sleep, and he raised his head, his brow furrowed and looked over at me.

"Hey," he murmured, and he reached over to put his hand on the small of my back. I leapt to my feet at once, as though he had pressed a hot iron there instead. Really, it was because his touch still made my heart rush a little faster in my chest, and after what I had found out, I knew I couldn't allow that to happen any longer.

"I think you should go," I told him firmly, and he pushed himself up on his elbow and looked at me, his brow furrowed.

"What's wrong?" He asked, his voice still a little blurry and gravelly from sleep. The covers slipped down his chest, to reveal that perfectly-hewn body. How could I have believed that it belonged to anything other than a young man? I cursed myself for being too quick to jump into bed with him. Maybe he would have come clean to me at some point if I had given him more time, but I hadn't, and now I was caught up in the middle of this huge mess and I had no clue how to get out of it.

Did I just come out and tell him what I knew? I would feel like a snoop for coming clean about it, but he could already tell that there was something wrong with me. Maybe I should just be honest. Maybe I should tell him that I knew that I didn't want him in my house a moment longer because I wasn't sure that I was going to be able to keep my hands off him if he didn't get the heck out of here...

"I think you should go," I told him quickly. I didn't want to have that conversation with him, not now, not yet. Probably not ever. I was just way too mortified to even think about the reality of what I had just done. He stared at me for a moment, and the corners of his mouth quirked up, as though he was sure I was joking.

"What?"

"I think you should probably get out of here," I repeated myself. It was the third time I had told him this, and if he didn't start paying attention soon, then I was going to kick up a fuss. I had to pull my eyes away from him, my body urging me to move back towards him, to kiss him the way that I really wanted to. It was absurd to think that just a few moments before, I had been considering sliding back into bed with him and going for another round. I had never taught him, but I had seen his face around school, and the whole thing was just making me feel seriously nasty.

"If that's what you want," He replied calmly, and he went to grab his clothes from next to the bed and got dressed. I held the robe that I had put on tight around me and prayed that he would get out soon and without too much protest.

He pulled on his clothes and turned back to me. Even fresh out of bed, with his hair a little messy from sleep and his stubble more prominent on his face, he was gorgeous. For a moment, I almost convinced myself that I had been overreacting to all of this, that I would explain it to him and he would back off and apologize and then we could move on.

But he had hidden something from me. Something important. Something that would have changed the way I went about this if I had known. He was younger than he said he was, by a good few years, and I had a connection to his family that I wasn't going to be able to shake just like that. This had been a bad idea. I would chalk it up to bad luck and move on, but I wasn't going to be able to do that until he got the heck out of my house.

"Are you going to tell me why?" he asked, and I thrust his phone into his hand. The last thing I wanted was for him to come crawling back later on looking for the damn thing. I shook my head.

"I'm sure you'll figure it out," I replied, and I opened the door.

"See you later?" He asked hopefully, and I shook my head.

"Please," I told him, putting on my best teacher voice to tell him to get out of there once and for all. There was no way that I could put up with having him around me for another second, not after what he had done. Just thinking about it made my entire body shiver like I had been dunked in cold water.

He raised his eyebrows and walked out the door, and he shot me one last look before I could close it. Without thinking, I darted forward and kissed him on the cheek; a learned response, if anything. I instantly regretted it. Well, not the chance to have been close to him again for a split second, but the fact that I had managed to send him yet another mixed message.

I closed the door quickly in his face and leaned up against it, listening until I could hear his footsteps heading down the stairs and away from me. Thank *God.* He was out of there. What a relief. Just being around him made my head feel like it was going to pop.

I couldn't believe I had let myself get involved with him, even for one night. I made a mental note to check out the family history of anyone that I got involved with. Nobody was going to slip through that net again, not a chance in hell. And I would put up the cut-off for my age range too, because if I hadn't let Mallory convince me to slide it down again, none of this would have happened in the first place. I should have stuck to my gut. I should have trusted that the old version of me knew just what she was doing.

In fact, term was back in just a couple of weeks. Maybe now was a good time to remind myself that I would have to get back into my old mindset. This new version of me had been a nice idea for a joke, for a laugh, for a hot minute, but I had better things to do with my time than sit around and pretend that I knew how to date again.

Because, clearly, I had no damn clue what I was doing when it came to that. Clearly I was just going to stumble into any number of ridiculous roadblocks until I gave up on it all again. Better to just jump forward a little in time and get over this whole little trip. It hadn't worked for me. I had tried a half-dozen dates now, and even the one that had gone well had actually gone badly – I just hadn't realized that until the morning after it had happened.

I shook my head at myself, pissed that I had allowed myself to feel anything at all for that man. For that boy, really. Just because he had talked the talk, walked the walk – just because he had fucked me better than anyone ever had in my entire life before...

I pushed that straight to the back of my head. None of that mattered. Not one part of that mattered anymore. Because I should never have been dumb enough to let it happen in the first place. I should never have let him into my bed and I knew it. I should have trusted the guy instinct inside me that told me to lay off, leave off, let us get to know each other a little better before we did anything like that, because God only knew how much I would have hated it if something like that came around to bite me in the ass again.

I went to make myself another coffee, but I found that my hands were shaking near-uncontrollably. I couldn't stop thinking about him, about the picture that I had seen on that phone, about the way it had made me feel to know that I had allowed myself to be misled like that. He must have known. He *must* have known. There was no way that this could have been a coincidence on his part, could it? He didn't just run into me by chance, and then have to figure out why I was booting him out of my house with a face like damn thunder.

I needed to talk to someone about this. I needed to make sure that I hadn't totally overreacted to what had happened between us. I had kissed him before he left and I knew that I was sending mixed signals but it was hard to care when I felt so mixed-up inside myself. One half of me wanted to just lay hands on him, drag him back inside the house, tell him that I had been wrong and that I wanted more and that I was sorry for jumping to such unflattering conclusions about him. The other half...

There was no way that I could tell anyone about any of this. Best to keep it to myself and hope that I could write it all out of existence, even inside my own head, too. I couldn't imagine sitting opposite one of my friends and coming clean about the way that I had climbed into bed with someone who had been a *student* until so recently – ugh, and he was so much younger than me too, I was practically a cradle-snatcher.

Suddenly, all the effort that I had put in to change myself, everything that I had done to try and make my life better, it seemed to fall apart in an instant. I couldn't do this anymore. It just wasn't who I was, not really, not when it came down to it. And look at the mess it had landed me in, trying to change who I was, trying to fit into some mould that I knew in my heart had never been made for me.

Time to go back to what I knew. Time to embrace who I really was. And time to forget that any of this had ever happened at all.

I could hardly wait to put it all behind me.

Chapter Eight

Do it in the classroom

As soon as I saw him standing outside the school gate, I knew that I was in trouble.

It had been three weeks since my date with Joseph, and I knew that he had been back on the rig for that time; what a relief, knowing that I didn't have to concern myself with running into him out and about. But still, the memory of what had happened that night was still heavy in my head, and I would have rather just forgotten about the whole thing.

I had spoken to Mallory about what had happened, because God only knew that I needed to get it off my chest; I shifted the age difference a little, just to make sure that I didn't seem like too much of a creep, and filled her in on the general details. She had listened, and it looked like her jaw was ready to drop off by the time I got to the end of it.

"You're actually serious," she asked, once I got to the end of the story. It wasn't phrased as a question, but more as a statement, as though she was convincing herself of the fact.

"Yeah," I agreed. "I know, it sounds crazy, but-"

"You kicked him out?" She asked. "You really kicked him out, even though it was that good between you?"

"It's not that simple-"

"I think you're just looking for a way to get out of being with someone," she told me bluntly. "It's been so long and you're still nervous about it, aren't you?"

I glanced away from her. In the time since he had left, that had crossed my mind, if I was being honest. I didn't like the thought that this was all sprung from some kind of self-protective measure, but I knew that it wouldn't have been so easy to justify if that was the case.

"I've just got to do what makes me feel right," I told her. "Listen to my gut, and all that."

"Just make sure your gut isn't trying to convince you that this is bad when there's nothing wrong with it," she pointed out. I consoled myself with the reminder that if she had actually known the truth of the age gap between us, she would hardly have been as happy about it; he was too young for me, that was for damn sure.

He wasn't that easy to get rid of, it seemed, much to my chagrin – I had hoped that he might take the hint and just back off and not make this difficult for me, but he reached out a couple of times, confused as to what had happened. Every time a message from him popped up onto my phone, I found myself torn – I wanted to reply to him and talk to him and let him know that I hadn't been able to stop thinking about him in all of this, for better or for worse, but I knew I couldn't. I had already sent enough mixed signals his way without having to throw that in on top of it.

I had kissed him. If I had just managed to resist the urge to kiss him then none of this would have happened in the first place. I would have kicked him out and he would have been confused about it but he would have accepted it because that was the kind of man that he was. He could have put it down to some crazy mixed signals and that would have been the end of it, and he would never have tried to pick up where we'd left off.

But no. Instead, I had left that door open for him, and he was determined to find some way to cut through it, because he wanted to see me again, and it was like nothing on this Earth was going to stop him from doing that if he got the chance.

I knew that if I'd told him to go fuck himself and never to speak to me again, that he would have left me alone and been done with me; he would have respected that much, at least. But I wasn't shooting him down – in fact, I wasn't saying much at all in response to his messages. I was just letting them pile up because I was far too nervous to think about the reality of actually saying *no* once and for all. I wasn't ready to close that door, even though I should have been.

I went back to school after the break more or less mortified with what had happened between me and that former student. I knew that if anyone other than Mallory was to catch wind of what had happened between us, every single person in the village would know within ten minutes. That was just how it worked around here, how it had always worked; keeping secrets was nigh-on impossible, especially when it was something as damn juicy as this. I was lucky that Mallory had always been such a loyal friend to me, because I needed to talk to someone about it but I knew I couldn't go dropping this on just anyone.

Every message I got from him was an assault on what I had tried to convince myself was the truth. That I didn't want him, that I didn't need him, that there was no part of him that would have made my life any better – only parts that would have made it worse. But whenever that face popped up on my phone, I felt that certainty waver. I wanted him. God only knew how much I wanted him. I needed to be with him, I needed to be close to him, I needed to feel him near me...

I couldn't stop thinking about the night that we had spent together. I had never felt so wanted in my entire life. I had been with a fair few guys in my time, but none, not one of them, had made me feel like that. It wasn't just that he knew what to do with his hands or his tongue or his cock, but that when he touched me it felt like he was worshiping every inch of me. I had never felt more desired in my entire life before, and that was dangerously enticing to me. After so long just hiding myself away and pretending that I had never even heard of having a libido, having him touch me like that had just been...well, it had made my heart ache and my body hurt for him, hurt for the need of him, hurt for the lack of him.

And so, I didn't cut things off. I just let those messages stack up, let him wait for a response, let him wonder what he was missing out on. And yeah, okay, maybe there was some part of me that enjoyed the attention that he was lavishing on me. It had been a long time since I had felt wanted by someone, and let alone someone who I actually wanted to want me to some degree, and the little boost I got every time he reached out to me was what I needed to keep me from cutting things off entirely. I knew that it wasn't exactly the nicest thing in the world, but he had lied to me about who he was - I wasn't going to go beating myself up too badly, given that he had held some pretty important stuff back when we'd first met.

And that was what I kept telling myself.

I didn't expect to see him again, at least not in person.

But I hadn't counted on how much he, apparently, wanted to see me again.

I was waiting by the gate and seeing all the kids off to their various buses and parents and lifts back home when I spotted him. He was dressed in dark jeans and a black t-shirt, not bothering with a jacket, and the sight of his arms made my heart swim with excitement.

And then, my stomach dropped. Just what the hell was he doing here? Joseph walked towards me, his eyes pinned to me as though he could see nobody else, and I felt everything around me slow down for a long moment as I tried to prepare for what I was going to say to him.

I had practiced a million times in my head the sharp telling-off that I had ready for him if I ever saw him again, but all of that seemed to just drift and drip away from my mind when I actually saw him standing there. It was one thing to be able to recite it in my head when there was nobody there to hear it, quite another to come out and tell it to him when he was standing there in person.

"Abigail," he greeted me with a nod, and to anyone else he could have passed for one of the dads flirting with me at the school gate. I had done it often enough, keeping them at arm's length and giving them just enough to keep the both of us entertained, but I had always felt like I was comfortably and completely in control. With him, with this, it was different. The world was tipping on its side, the ground threatening to slip-slide out from under me, and the only thing keeping me on my feet was his eyes, those eyes that made everything around me slow down.

"What are you doing here?" I asked, hoping that how much he had thrown me wasn't evident on my face. I doubted I was doing much of a good job at hiding it. I glanced around, making sure that nobody had seen us talking; I wanted to be able to deny that I had ever seen him here, as though that would make all of this go away somehow.

"I'm here to pick up my sister," he replied. "Mary. Mum's busy this afternoon and I don't get to see so much of Mary since I'm offshore so much."

It was a good story, but I knew it was only half the truth. At least part of the reason that he was here was because of me. He knew this was where to find me, how to scare an answer to all those messages out of me. I had been the one in control for a little too long for his liking, and now he was claiming that back from me and I had no choice but to give him an answer.

Seeing him like this, it sent all those feelings that I had tried to pin down inside of me rushing back through my head. I hated this. I loved it. I was so happy to see him, and I was so scared that I was going to give something away by just being close to him like this, too. My body ached, my skin prickled, and I could remember so vividly the way that his hands had felt when they had moved all over my body. I could remember his tongue between my legs, could remember the way he made my back arch when I came. And I knew, from the look in his eyes, that he could remember it all, too.

"I don't think you should come here when I'm working," I told him bluntly, but there was a waver in my voice that gave him all the space he needed to stay.

"Why not?" He replied. "You scared you won't be able to handle yourself around me?"

I glanced around, making sure that nobody had heard him speak those words to me. My heart was pounding dangerously fast in my chest and it felt like my blood was on fire in my veins, but the feeling was, somehow, good. Like this was what my body had been built for.

"Come inside," I ordered him. I couldn't do this out here. I couldn't risk it - I didn't want people to see us together for more than a moment, and I knew that if Mallory caught a single glimpse of us, then she would never let me forget it. He raised his eyebrows at me, and I ignored what he was trying to tell me with them. I didn't care. He needed to get out of there, and I needed to feel him closer to me, and I could only think of one way to answer those problems for both of us.

I took him back to my classroom – mercifully empty, thank all things good and pure – and closed the door behind him. I crossed my arms over my chest and turned my attention to him.

"What are you really doing here?" I asked.

"You wouldn't answer my messages," he told me bluntly. "And I know that you want to. I thought you might find it a little easier to say what you need to say in person."

I looked away from him. I couldn't tell him the truth. I couldn't tell him how much I knew. But my God, standing there, so close to him, the burning, pulsing chemistry between us was nearly impossible to deny. And maybe I didn't want to deny it for another moment.

Before I could stop myself, I moved towards him, planted a kiss on his lips. I knew this was stupid, knew this was crazy, and knew above all else that if anyone caught wind of what we were doing in here then I would land myself in some serious hot water. But then, his hands came to my waist and he pushed me back against my desk and I knew that I had made the right choice. How could it be the wrong one, when it brought me closer to him?

His tongue was in my mouth at once, his lips parting mine, our bodies coming together just like they had back at my flat. I couldn't believe that I had managed to hold off of him for so long – not when being near him like this felt so good. All those questions I'd had, all that fear and panic that I was doing something wrong or that I had done something wrong or that I was about to ruin my life, they fell away at once. How could they matter when this man was touching me?

Something fell from the desk, but I didn't care, didn't have the attention span to focus on picking it up again. There were large windows in the room that looked out onto the back playground, and if someone happened to be wandering through them, they would have seen us kissing on the desk and my cover would have been blown. But something about the thought of getting caught just made this all the more thrilling to me. Who was I? Who was this version of me that came out when he was around? Was this the version that I had been looking for when I had tried to switch things up, to change things for the better?

I would have fucked him right there. I really would. And I wouldn't have given a damn what happened or who saw or what they would have thought of me when they did. None of that mattered one little bit in my head, not when I was kissing him, not when his strong arms were around me. He hitched me up onto the desk and I spread my legs and hooked them around him. The libido that I had tried to pretend didn't exist since my ex had left me was back and it wasn't going to be ignored a moment longer. He moved his mouth to my neck and I gasped and moaned and-

And suddenly realized what I was doing.

I pushed him away from me firmly, pulling my gaze from him, hating myself for letting it get this far – why couldn't I resist him? I was a grown-up woman and I had control over what I did and who I did it with, but when I was around him, all of that just seemed to stop, to fall away.

"What is it? What's wrong?" Joseph asked. His eyes were dark and his breath was coming harder and faster than it had before, and I knew that it was as hard for him to bring this to such a sudden halt as it was for me.

"You need to get out of here," I told him, echoing my words when he had been back at the flat with me. He furrowed his brow.

"Why? I don't-"

"You don't need to," I told him, closing my eyes and rubbing my hand over my face, trying to wipe the memory of how good it had been to kiss him from my mind.

"You just need to go," I ordered him. "Get out of the school. Please. I can't be around you. It's not...it's not good for me. It's not..."

I couldn't find the words. Safe? Maybe that had something to do with it. I felt like I was on the brink of being exposed when I was around him. But it was more than that. I felt this loss of control, a control that I had fought so hard for for so long, but when I was with him, it just stopped existing. I wasn't going to risk that. I couldn't risk that.

He stared at me for a long moment, as though he was giving me time to change my mind, and I just kept my eyes away from him and hoped that he would go without too much of a fuss. Finally, and with a long sigh, he turned and slowly walked out of the classroom, as though he could hardly believe that I was doing this to him. I closed my eyes. It was the only way that I could let him leave without stopping and cracking and begging him to come back. I hated that I was so weak-willed, but there was nothing that I could do to change the way I felt around him – the way I felt when I was close to him, and the way that he made me feel like the whole world was on the brink of changing around me.

The door opened again and my eyes sprang open, but it was only Mallory, slipping into the classroom to drop off some folder inserts that she had promised me. I quickly pulled down my skirt and hoped that I didn't look too ruffled – double-hoped that she hadn't spotted Joseph making his way on out of here.

"Hey," I greeted her, busying myself with picking up what we had knocked off the desk.

"Hey, are you alright?" She asked. "I thought you were meant to be doing the gate today..."

"I was," I replied. "I just needed to grab something from in here, that's all. I'm heading back out now, don't worry."

"I wasn't trying to get on you," she remarked. "Just wondering..."

"I'm fine," I told her again, and I knew that if I said another word, she was going to be on to me.

So, instead of hanging around and waiting to get busted, I headed for the door, brushed past her, and headed back out to the gate to do my duty. And prayed, above all else, that Joseph wasn't going to make himself any more of a problem today than he already had.

Chapter Nine

Just to be close to you

As soon as I heard the engine sputtering below me, I felt a wave of dread slide through me. Fuck. *Fuck.* I knew that I should have taken this damn thing in to get serviced sooner rather than later. And now, I was paying the price for it.

I managed to pull in at the side of the Loch before the engine gave out completely. I groaned as I slid to a slow halt, and silently cursed myself for thinking that I could keep this thing going when it had been telling me that I needed to get it checked up for ages now.

It had been a hell of a long day – I had been out at a teacher training conference thing, and by the time that I got off to head back home, it was starting to get dark. I had just wanted to get back to my place and put my feet up and be done with this whole mess, but instead, I was going to have to call out a mechanic in the middle of the night and hope for the best...

Not that I imagined I would have much luck finding someone who would do the job with me at this time of the evening. It was nearing nine, and most of them would have shut up shop a while ago. Which meant that I was going to have to go outside the normal range of services I might have employed, and look at something a little more...

No. I couldn't call him up. There was no way. I hadn't spoken to Joseph since we'd had that encounter in my classroom a few days ago, and there was a good reason for that; I was totally and utterly done with the very thought of having him around. I needed to be. For my own sanity, for my own peace of mind. I had to let go.

But who else was going to be around at this time of night who would be able to help with my car? Truth was, I couldn't think of one person who would have been willing to turn out to the middle of nowhere, who would have the knowledge on top of that to actually be of any use to me. He was an engineer, after all, he would know what he was doing. If there was anyone I could use the help from...

Maybe I was just looking for an excuse to see him again. I hadn't been able to stop *thinking* about him since we had shared that little moment in the classroom. There had been something so outrageously hot about knowing that we could have been caught at any moment, and yet not caring enough to stop because we were just that much into one another. There weren't words for how much I felt like I needed him. And we had left that chapter still open, and I wasn't sure that I could cope with just not seeing him again even when I knew that what I needed more than anything was some distance, space, time to get my head straight.

I had kept what had happened to myself. It was just safer that way. I didn't want anyone knowing what was going on. If anyone even caught wind of this, then there would be serious trouble – I couldn't imagine the mess that would come up if it was public knowledge that I was sleeping with an ex-student at the school I taught at, not to mention the fact that his little sister was still a pupil there, too.

But I still had his number in my phone. I had kept it there, for reasons that even I hadn't been able to fully justify to myself, for a long-ass time now. And there had to be something behind it, some reason that the universe had made me hang on to it. Maybe it was because someone up there knew that I was going to need some emergency mechanics late on a cool Autumn evening and that he was just the man to give them to me?

It felt like the set-up to some porn movie. Maybe that's what he would take it as. *Fuck it.* I couldn't sit here on the side of the road for the rest of the night for want of someone less awkward to contact. I was going to call him. Get it over with.

I dialed his number and a moment later he picked up the phone, as though he had been waiting to hear from me.

"Hello?"

"Hey, Joseph?" I greeted him, and I took a deep breath. There was still time for me to back all the way out of this conversation if I wanted to, but I wasn't sure that I did. I could have just hung up and pretended that I hadn't meant to call him up. But I did. I needed to hear his voice. I needed to hear those words, honeyed, dripping into my ear. I didn't care how I got them or where they came from, but I needed them, something ferocious, something fierce.

"I'm stuck in the layby at the side of the Loch," I explained. "You know, the one down from Arpafeelie?"

"What's wrong?" He asked, sounding worried at once. "Why are you stuck there?"

"My car broke down," I replied. "I don't know how to fix it. I was hoping..."

"I'll be there in twenty," he told me at once, and with that, he hung up the phone, and left me sitting there in the car with a slight smile on my face, pleased that he was already in such a hurry to see me once more.

It didn't even take him the full twenty minutes he had told me to have him arrive right there to help me; he pulled over his car, something sleek and classic that he had told me he'd worked on to pull it back up to scratch, and gestured for me to roll the window down.

"Hey," he greeted me, with a broad smile. "You mind getting out? Let me take a look at this thing for you..."

"Of course," I replied, and I slipped out of the car and gestured for him to go right ahead and take a look. I leaned on the side of the car and watched him and wondered how this made him feel. Was he feeling a little off-put by the fact that I had just hit him up out of nowhere to ask for his help? If he was, he was certainly doing a good job hiding it. He hardly seemed bothered at all. It didn't take long until he had popped the hood of the car and stuck his head underneath, and he emerged a moment or two later, looking grim.

"It doesn't look great," he remarked. "I have a friend I can call if you'd like me to-"

"No, it's fine," I replied, waving my hand. "I just want to get back. I have insurance on this thing, I just need to call them up and I know they'll fix it for me."

He paused for a moment, eyeing me. I knew exactly what was going through his mind. I looked him in the eye, daring him to say it.

"Can I give you a lift back to your place?" He offered, and I smiled.

"Sure," I agreed, and he led me to his car, opening the door for me, helping me inside. What the fuck was I doing? I should have told him no, shot him down, got on with my life. But I couldn't shake him. Couldn't shake the want for him. Couldn't shake my need to come for him, no matter what it took, no matter how much of a mess we knew that it would land us in.

"You know, I didn't expect to hear from you," he remarked, as he pulled out of the layby and back onto the road.

"I didn't expect to be calling you," I admitted. And it was the truth, at least some of it; he had been the last person I'd expected to get in touch with today. Though I had woken up thinking of him. Though I had dreamed of him the night before, lain in bed and imagined what it would have been like to have him next to me once more. Remembered, with a such vividness, the passion that he had brought to my bed, even if it was just for one night. I needed him. I craved him. Something deep down in my guts made it impossible for me to resist or forget about him, no matter how much I wanted to.

But my brain, that logical part, told me that we could never be anything more than friends. Because if someone found out about us, then there would be trouble. One time, well, I could put that down to a bad decision, nothing more than that, but more than once, when I was knowing about everything that he was to me, that would have just been in bad taste.

He pulled up outside my block of flats, and I took a deep breath. I wanted to tell him to go, but that seemed a little mean, given that he had come in and played my hero when I had needed him to.

"Do you want a drink?" I asked him. "A cup of tea, I mean?"

"I would love that," he agreed.

"But no funny business, alright?" I warned him. I knew that it was a cliché, but he needed to know that nothing was going to happen between us; he needed to know that this was where it ended.

"I'll see what I can do," he replied, and he helped me out of the car and we headed up the steps together once again.

It was hard not to think of the first time that he had come up to my flat when we had slept together for the first time. When I had kissed him in the street, and everything else had fallen away. And I could convince myself that this man, this perfect man, was the one that I was meant to be with.

I turned on the kettle when I got in, and he sank into the living room couch and looked around.

"You've been here before," I reminded him.

"Yeah, but I didn't get much of a chance to see anything outside the bedroom," He reminded me. I couldn't help but smile. I was doing my best not to think about what had happened between us then. But then the kettle pinged and I made us a couple of cups of tea, and I went to the living room to give it to him.

"Thanks for coming out and helping me tonight," I murmured.

"Well, it wouldn't be very gentlemanly to leave you out there alone," he replied.

"Guess I gave you the chance to be a gentleman," I teased him.

"Lucky that you don't know many engineers," He remarked. I cocked my head at him.

"What makes you think that you're the only engineer I know?" I shot back. "Maybe I have a whole little black book of them."

"But you called me, huh?"

"Maybe I tried everyone else first and you were the only one I could get to..."

"Maybe I need to make myself your go-to in future," he replied. He moved a little closer to me, and I froze on the spot – I didn't know what to think. But there was a chemistry between us, my body aching for his touch. I could still remember how good it felt to kiss him, the power of the way his body felt against mine.

"Hey, don't worry," he murmured, and he slowly eased my shoes off my feet. I didn't move – I smiled and wriggled my toes in my tights.

"You had a long day?" He asked. I nodded.

"Teacher training," I replied, knowing that this was dangerous, this was getting far too close to breaking the rules that I had set up for myself. He took one foot in his hands and began to slowly massage me, going gentle, going slow but firm. It was exactly how he had been when we had been in bed together. His fingers kneaded my muscles, and I closed my eyes and let my head rest back against the couch.

"You're good at that," I remarked.

"Yeah, well, I'm good at a lot of things," he reminded me. He was flirting, outrageously, but I supposed I was the one who had called him up this night, I was the one who had invited him up here, I was the one who had allowed him to put his hands on me and touch me. I was the one who was letting this happen. And I was the one who wanted it to happen.

"I remember," I replied, and I took a deep breath. I reached for my tea and he picked up my other foot and started to work on it. I loved the way he looked at my body when he touched me, loved the way it made me feel when he took hold of me. I couldn't help but smile as I watched him.

"What are you grinning about?" He asked. There was this strange mix of sensation between us at that moment; both tension and relaxation, something that existed between the two so that I couldn't tell the difference between them. I wasn't even sure that it was important I did anymore. All that mattered was that he was here and that he was touching me and that at last I could just let myself be around him again, be around him the way that I knew I needed to.

"I don't know," I admitted. "I don't really know what to think right now."

"What do you mean?"

"I mean..." I trailed off, trying to find the words to tell him what I needed to and coming up with a fresh blank. I shook my head.

"It's nothing."

"Tell me," he told me, squeezing my feet in his hands lightly, sending pleasurable shivers up my spine. It wasn't arousal, not quite, nothing that obvious – something softer, sweeter. Just the way he had been all night long.

"I just like being around you," I admitted. "But I don't...I don't think I should."

"Why do you feel like that?" He asked with curiosity.

"Because of how old you are," I told him. "And the fact that you lied to me about your age. And that you used to go to my school. And that your sister still does go there."

"None of that stuff matters-"

"It does to me," I told him firmly. "It might not to you, but it does to me. I can't just brush it off that easily. I wish I could, trust me, but it's not so easy."

"Why not?"

"People judge," I explained. "You know that. You've lived in this town your whole life, you get it."

"Who cares if they judge?" He asked, and his hand slipped an inch further up my leg; I gently brushed him back, telling him without words that I didn't want him to touch me like that, not until I knew for sure how I felt about it.

"I do," I reminded him. "I do, because it might be enough to get in the way of my job, remember? I don't want anyone talking behind my back, especially not the parents of the kids I'm involved with."

"So we make sure they don't talk about us," he suggested. "We don't give them anything to talk about."

"You're not doing a very good job at that, given that you turned up at the school recently," I pointed out to him. He grinned and held his hands up.

"Hey, what can I say, I just knew I had to see you..."

"Yeah, seems like you have trouble controlling yourself," I fired back, half-kidding.

"When it comes to you, you better believe it," he replied, and his voice was low and sure and made something in me stir to life. I ignored it.

"Why?" I asked.

"Why what?" He replied, raising his eyebrows at me.

"Why do you want to be with me so much?" I asked, and I was more than a little nervous of the answer. "I mean...you could have any woman at all that you wanted, you have to know that. There isn't a girl in this town who would turn you down if you gave her the chance to get to know you."

"I want you," he replied, as though it should have been obvious. My heart skipped a beat.

"I've had a crush on you since high school," he explained, working on my feet once more, pulling his gaze from mine for a moment.

"I was always pissed that I didn't end up in any of your classes, but I guess I can see that's a good thing now," he remarked. "You would have recognized me right away."

He took a deep breath, and then carried on.

"I always had a thing for older women, after I saw you back then," he remarked. "That's why I had the age range set higher on my dating profile. I was always looking for someone like you. And then I saw you turn up on the page and I thought – I thought it must have been a mistake or something. When you actually started talking to me and you agreed to meet with me and all of that, it was like a dream come true. Really. You have no idea how long I've dreamed about..."

He had to catch himself before he went any further, and I had to catch myself before I asked him to keep going and tell me just what he had been thinking about me all that time. I knew that it was crazy, but I loved the idea of him fantasizing about me. I had never been someone's fantasy girl before but I could tell from the way that he looked at me that he wasn't making this up, that he truly felt that passionately about me. How hot was it to know that you were someone's ultimate one-day dream? It was enough to make my head spin. No wonder every moment with him felt so precious; that was just how he was treating it, too.

"And I want you to know, even if you never want anything else to do with me again," he continued. "I'm here. I'm not going anywhere. I've got your back."

"You mean that?" I asked softly. It had been far too long since someone had said that to me and I had actually believed it; normally, I was the one people had on their back burner, ready to tap into when they needed me. Not their first choice. Not the girl they came to when they had an option to go elsewhere.

"I really mean that," he murmured. "I mean, don't get me wrong, sleeping with you for the first time, that was pretty fucking incredible. But I'm here if you don't want to do that, or if you do. I know you can feel something between us just the way that I can, but I'm not going to push it, Abi. It's all on your terms. I want you to know that."

I gazed at him in silence for a long moment. I had no idea what to say to what he had just told me. I wanted to throw my arms around him and thank him for saying the words out loud that I had never known I needed to hear, but that would have been too much too soon.

"Will you stay here?" I asked him, without thinking. "Tonight?"

"You want me to stay?" He asked, and he seemed surprised. His hands stilled on my feet for a moment, but I could still feel their comforting warmth through my stockings. I nodded.

"I don't think we should...I mean, I don't want to have sex," I told him. It was only somewhat true, of course – I wanted to slide into bed with him and see what he could do with that amazing body of his once more, but I knew that I had too much to figure out on my own terms before that happened again.

"That's fine," he assured me. "Anything you want, remember? I mean that."

I smiled at him. He was so warm and genuine, in a way no man I had ever been with had been before. Just the way he touched me, the way he talked to me, the way he bared his soul to me, he was making it clear that he had nothing to hide. I liked that. Made me feel safe around him. Like anything could have happened, but he had me rooted safely to the ground where I belonged.

"Let me make you something to eat," he suggested. "If you haven't had dinner yet, I don't want you to be going hungry because of me..."

And with that, he got to his feet, gently laying my legs down on the couch, and headed through to the kitchen. I didn't even know what I had in there, but the fact that he didn't even wait for my okay, the fact that he was so keen to look after me – that was something profound.

I lay there on the couch and watched him as he went to work, taking care of dinner for us, cooking something quick and light – some pasta dish that he managed to construct from the store cupboard bare essentials that I had kicking around. I knew there wasn't much there, but he whipped up something impressive in no time. It was amazing what this man could do when I gave him the space to flourish. Maybe I should have taken that as more of an indicator of what he was capable of.

When he was done, he brought me out a bowl of steaming pasta drenched in a healthy serving of a thick, rich tomato sauce. It smelled fantastic, and my mouth watered as soon as he handed it to me.

"This looks great," I told him, and I inhaled deeply as it arrived in my hands. "Where did you learn to cook like this?"

"Mum taught me," he replied. "She didn't want me going out into the world not knowing how to take care of myself, that's all."

"That makes a change from every other man I've dated," I laughed, and he cocked an eyebrow at me.

"Dated?"

I glanced away from him quickly. I couldn't let him, or myself, think of it like that. It was far too dangerous. I needed to gather myself, keep myself together, remind myself that this was never going to happen and that he was just here because he was doing me a favor.

We ate together, and we talked a little – about nothing in particular, his work, my work, what had dragged me out of my warm bed to be out in the middle of nowhere like that. I was tired, but being with him, it made me feel like I had been shot through with a warm, bright energy. Like I could have taken on the world in that moment. I wondered if he felt it, too. I wondered if he felt as alive as I did when we were close to each other.

By the time that I had finished the meal he'd made for me, my belly was full and I could feel myself getting sleepy. But I didn't want him to go. I knew that I should have gotten rid of him by now, should have told him to leave, but with every minute that passed, it seemed like he was better-suited to being here. Like he was what this place had been lacking all along.

"I probably should head to bed," I remarked, and I eyed him, giving him space to excuse himself and leave before anything happened. I was relying on him to draw the line there, because I knew that I didn't have it in me to do that. Not when I knew that he was so damn good in bed.

"Can I come with you?" He asked simply. I opened my mouth to correct him, but he was quick to fill in the blanks himself.

"No sex, I know," he assured me. "I just want to be close to you, Abi."

I couldn't help but smile when he told me that. I knew that this was probably just asking for trouble, but I had already done that when I had called him up in the first place. I might as well have just allowed myself to go the extra mile and actually sleep next to someone that I wanted to wake up beside.

"Just sleeping," I warned him again, and he nodded and smiled.

"Of course," he promised me, and I knew that he meant it. I knew that I could have put any rules in place at all here and he would have abided by them in an instant. That was just who he was when he was around me; he listened to me, took me seriously. He knew that he had already pushed his luck practically as far as it would go with what he had done in keeping the truth from me, and that meant that I got to call every shot now that we were actually...well, together was the wrong word. But close. In the same room once more.

I went for a shower, and he offered to clear up after dinner; Jesus, as though this man couldn't get any more perfect. I let the hot water run over me and swore to myself that I wasn't going to let anything else happen tonight. Not until I'd had some more time to think on it, figure out if it was right or not – there was some part of me, some not-small part of me, that found the thought of sharing a bed with him and not laying hands on him utterly impossible. But I could do it. I wanted to do it. I had the self-control to make this happen.

I changed into the most comfortable and non-sexy flannel pajamas that I had in my collection, and I headed through to the bedroom; he was already under the covers in my bed. His clothes were on the floor, all but his boxers; I supposed that I couldn't expect him to sleep fully-dressed, but the thought of his nakedness under those covers waiting for me was almost more than I could handle.

I slipped into the bed beside him, not touching him, making a point not to get too close. It would have just been dangerous; I felt like I could feel this heat rolling off him in waves, drawing me to him, a warning and a temptation all at the same time. His skin seemed to pulse with energy and I wished I could lean in and feel it, feel it against mine again. I wondered if he was thinking the same thing.

"Thanks for letting me stay tonight," he murmured, his soft voice breaking the silence.

"Thanks for saving me when it came to the car," I replied, and I smiled. The tension seemed to leave between us; we could do this. We had to prove it to each other, that this was more than just the raw physical attraction. I needed to be able to trust that there was something else to this. That this wasn't just the rawness that I had seen it as when we had first climbed into bed together.

I reached for his hand beneath the covers. My heart was pounding. I wrapped my fingers around his, and he held on to them tight, as though he never wanted to let me go. *See?* I could do this. Being close to him was easy. It was fun. It could just be the two of us and I wouldn't give in to all those base instincts that were screaming at me to do something, do something, do something.

And that's how I fell asleep that night. Just touching him.

Nothing else happened, as I had promised myself that it wouldn't; nothing else happened, because it didn't have to. Just the two of us being so close to each other was all that we needed to feel alive, to feel the passion.

Much as I would have liked to be able to dismiss all of this as a fling, as nothing more than an attraction, I could feel now that it was so much more than that. Because, as I slept, I dreamed of nothing. Nothing that my mind could come up with was better than this.

And so, I just rested, next to the man I knew now that I was falling for. And there was nothing I could do to stop this in its tracks.

Chapter Ten

Time to say goodbye

"WELL, YOU KNOW WHAT you need to do, right?"

When Mallory said that to me, once I had filled her in on everything that was going on with Joseph, I couldn't help but furrow my brow. I had no clue how to handle any of it, and here she was, coming at me like it should have been obvious.

"Do I?" I replied, and she nodded.

"You need to sleep with him again."

"What!"

I exclaimed the word so loudly that half the coffee shop we were in turned to see what all the fuss was about. I lowered my gaze, fixed my eyes on her once more.

"You can't be serious," I muttered, and she shrugged.

"That's the only way to get it out of your head," she replied. "Only way to stop wondering if you could have made something work between you. One more time, and then it's over and done with for good."

I leaned back in my seat and took a moment to ponder on what she had just said. It was a lot to take in, that was for sure, but maybe she actually had a point?

Ever since the night that Joseph had come around to my place and the two of us had shared the bed together and he had held me all night long, I had known that shaking him wasn't going to be easy. I was falling for him, hard, and I knew that he would have done anything to be with me. Knowing that someone wanted me so deeply and intently was a little dizzying, if I was being honest with myself, and it was addictive knowing that he valued me so highly.

And I had eventually come to Mallory and spilled the truth to her about what had been going on – that I couldn't shake him from my head, that I felt like I was going crazy without him, but that I knew that I wasn't going to be able to commit to him, not really. Not when I thought about everything that he had kept from me. Not when I thought about how people would react if they found out the truth of our relationship with one another. This town was the small, judgemental kind, and I knew better than to throw anything to those dogs that could have affected the way that they all saw me at work.

Now, though, she was telling me the last thing I needed to hear. That I should sleep with him again. I thought it was crazy, but then, I hadn't had much experience in actually getting over someone without a long-term relationship having taken place first. And then when that happened, everyone came crowding around you to make sure that you were okay, to take care of you, to give you all the space you needed to make yourself better. But this – I had slept with him once, and spent a couple of nights with him, and he had held something back about himself that would have changed everything. It wasn't exactly what most people would have thought of as something that needed getting over. And yet – and yet, I knew that I wasn't going to be able to hide from it. To hold back from it. I needed to see him again, needed to shake him once and for all. Now, I just had to figure out how the hell I was meant to do that.

Maybe she had a point. Maybe this was what I needed to get him out of my head once and for all. I mean, I had heard wilder propositions, that was for sure. I knew that I couldn't just cut him out, much as that was what would have made the most sense; I had to see him again, even just to confirm to myself that this was truly over between us.

"How does that work?" I asked, waving my hand to signal for Mallory to go on.

"Well, if you don't see him again, then you're going to spend all this time thinking about what *could* have happened between you, right?" She pointed out. "If you see him one last time, then you don't have to think about that. You know what happens because you did it. And then you can just move on."

I chewed my lip. It seemed distinctly dangerous to invite him back into my house again. I felt like it could only end in disaster, all things considered. But I would have been lying if I'd said that there wasn't some part of me that craved it. I had been looking for an excuse to get close to him again, and maybe that was just the kind that I had wanted.

I pondered on what Mallory had said to me for the rest of the week; we were back at school and I was glad to have classes back as a distraction. The dads still flirted with me at the school gate, and I told myself that I had my mojo back and then some – but I still found myself scanning to see if Joseph was anywhere to be seen.

I didn't want to see him, but I did.

It was a confusing place to be, the inside of my brain, and I wished I could figure it out one way or another.

Mallory had a point, though. Everything in there, at the moment, was clouded by the memories of how good it had been to sleep with him that first time around. I couldn't shake that. I needed to feel his touch again. That was the only way that I was going to be able to get all of this out of my head, I was sure of it.

And maybe it wouldn't even be as good this time around. Right? It couldn't have the same passion that it did the first time we had been in bed together. That had been all about the thrill of what we didn't know, and now that we had a better grasp on one another, that was going to fall away just like that. I was certain of it.

So certain I was, that I decided it was time to see him again. One last time. To get him out of my system for good. I was ready.

I texted him to tell him to come around to my place that Friday evening; I decided that I had to do this sooner rather than later if I was going to go through with it without backing out and panicking and changing my mind. He replied at once, told me he would be there, and asked if he wanted me to bring around a bottle of wine. I told him no. I wanted to be totally and utterly sober for this, to see if the chemistry was really there – or if I had managed to invent it with my tipsiness the first night we had been together.

It was funny, I felt like I was doing everything that I could to make this *not* work. Stacking all the cards against us to make sure that it hadn't just been the drink or the night or the shock of having a man want me that had tipped me to crave him so badly. I was trying to make sure that none of it had been a fluke, basically, trying to make sure that nothing led me to believe there was something there when I knew there was nothing.

But, of course, I still found myself rubbing lotion on to my legs, applying a little light make-up, changing the sheets, lighting a candle; if this was going to be the last time that I was with him, then I wanted to make damn sure that I didn't look back and regret a thing.

I made it home from work in record time that evening, and I cleaned up the place one last time and looked at myself in the mirror. This was going to be it. When this was over, I was moving on with my life. I wasn't going to let him or the memory of him get in the way of anything else that I wanted to do.

From this point forward, I was over him. I just had this one little stopover on the way.

When I opened the door, all my thoughts fell out of my head, and I just sank into his arms and let him kiss me once more.

I hadn't told him that this was meant to be the last time for us, but the way he kissed me, it was like he already knew. Like he had to give everything to this moment and not hold a damn thing back. I pulled him over the threshold to the apartment and felt my entire body sag with relief, like this was all I had been waiting for all this time. How had I managed to pretend, even for an instant, that this wasn't what I needed? Having him close to me once more, it was everything I had wanted, everything I had needed. There was no room or space or time for words, not when I needed his mouth, his sweet mouth, on mine once more...

"Fuck, I haven't been able to stop thinking about you," he murmured to me, clasping my face in his hands and gazing into my eyes like he could hardly believe that I was actually right there in front of him. I slipped my hand beneath the thin black t-shirt that he was wearing and felt the strength of his body beneath it. *Fuck.* I didn't know how I had managed to lie in bed next to him that whole night through and not just go crazy knowing what he was holding back from me.

"I need you to fuck me," I told him. I didn't have time to wait. I didn't have time to put it into any more words than that. I just needed him. Rough, hard, soft, slow, anything and any way he wanted to give it to me.

He scooped me up off the ground and carried me to the kitchen, planting me down on the counter, spreading my legs hungrily. I hadn't bothered with underwear that day, knowing that he was going to be inside me soon enough if I had my way. Honestly, getting dressed for this had been so hot to me, knowing that everything I put on, he was going to rip straight off of me. He seemed barely-contained when he was around me, like it took everything that he had to hold back and not just pin me down and take me right where I stood.

He cupped his hand around my pussy, and I felt the warmth of his fingers there, just for a moment. He felt incredible. I couldn't help but moan into his mouth, and he bared his teeth and bit down on my bottom lip. I hoped he would leave a mark. I wanted to remember this, remember every detail of this, commit it to memory where it belonged.

"Condom?" He demanded, and there was a rough edge to his voice that told me that this wasn't up for debate. I grabbed the one that I had tucked into the pocket of my skirt and pressed it into his hand. I didn't have words anymore, just need, just lust, just want for him, him, only him. My brain and body had agreed on this, for a change, agreed that this was what we needed, and I wasn't going to hold back now that I had him just where I wanted him.

He unzipped his trousers and sheathed himself quickly, and put one arm around my waist to draw me close. His eyes were on fire and his lips were slightly parted, as though there was something that he wanted to say to me but that he couldn't quite find the words to speak. I knew how he felt. There was so much I wanted to tell him but I had no idea where to start with any of it. It felt impossible, the weight of everything I needed to tell him, and I forced myself to hold it back for now. It didn't matter. None of it did. Nothing did, not until he was inside me once more.

And finally, he gave me what I had been craving so dearly. He drove himself deep into me in one, long thrust, and I clung to him and let him move inside me for the first time in what felt like forever. I couldn't believe I had managed to wait so long to get what I had needed so badly from him; fuck, it felt like every nerve-ending in my body was coming alive as he moved into me, over and over again, driving himself deep, filling me up to the very brim until I felt like there wasn't a thing more that I could take. I wrapped my legs around him and drew him into me as far and deep as he would go. I couldn't get enough. I couldn't even imagine getting enough. At the back of my mind, the memory that this was meant to help me get over him flickered through my head; I ignored it. It didn't work like that, not for us. I knew that I was meant to be using this to free myself from my connection to him, but I knew, utterly and surely in that moment, that this was just going to make it harder.

And I didn't want to stop. I didn't care that this was a bad idea. I didn't care anymore. I just needed him. My pussy had been aching for him for long enough now and now that I had him where I wanted him, where I needed him, nothing was going to stop me. I wrapped my arms around him, digging my nails into his back, and I buried my face into his shoulder and inhaled the scent of his aftershave. I would have bathed in this stuff just for the connection that it had to him in my head. How could anyone not fall at his feet? Everything about him was so utterly, totally edible; I wanted to consume him, every inch of him, make it so that nobody else could say that he was theirs. I was territorial over him and we had only spent a few nights together. That was the alchemy that existed between us, impossible to deny, impossible to hide from. I knew that, even if I could have, I wouldn't have tried. I needed him. Needed this.

I could feel him moving inside of me, and I couldn't remember a time in my life when being fucked like this had felt so good. Normally I had needed something before or during that would get me close, but being with him now, that was it. A raw, animal attraction that made every logical part of my brain switch off and slide into second gear. He turned his head to kiss me again, his tongue deep in my mouth, and I moaned helplessly. He knew just what he was doing to me. And he loved it.

"Fuck, you're so wet," he growled into my ear, and it was this version of Joseph that really drove me utterly crazy – the version of him that dropped the pretense of the sweet, kind, loving guy, and unleashed the animal within. The animal that I was quite sure I was the only one who got to see. I could already feel my pussy tingling, that fire in my belly that had been brewing since I had invited him out here in the first place threatening to grow and burst and consume us both. My toes curled in my shoes and they slipped to the floor with a clatter, and I didn't pay a moment of attention to them.

"You going to cum for me, Abi?" He murmured in my ear. There was almost a taunting edge to his voice, as though he knew how helpless I was in his hold. The low growl of it rolled through me, and he moved deeper, holding himself there, grinding himself deep inside of me, letting me get lost to the feeling of being taken by him, utterly and completely.

And I gave in. I couldn't hold back any longer. Everything that I had been holding on to, that control, at least, the idea of it, fell away from me at once and I felt my pussy contract around him. I couldn't stop myself from crying out, and he held himself there, letting me pulse around him, letting me take the last of his pleasure from him. It didn't take long until he had found his own release deep inside of me, and he groaned as he filled me with his seed, rocking slowly back and forth as he took the last of me for himself.

By the time that he pulled out of me, I was glad that he had planted me up on the counter because if he hadn't, I was sure that I would have just slipped straight down onto the floor in a great big puddle of pleasure. I couldn't think straight, couldn't open my mouth, all I could do was keep myself propped up and wait for my jaw to stop shaking and my teeth to stop chattering.

He pulled the condom off and disposed of it quickly, and then lifted me off the counter and into his arms. He was so strong, and it made me feel so safe when I was with him in this way, like I could have spent a lifetime in his arms and never had to fear for anything as part of it. He smiled as he planted me down on the couch, and I sank back into the welcoming embrace of the soft pillows.

"That was..." I tried to find the words to tell him how I felt. I couldn't. I supposed they weren't important, not really – all that mattered was the way that he was looking at me, as he sank down to the couch to join me again. He cupped my face in his hands and kissed me once more, and even though he had just pulled out of me, I felt that tingle deep down in my guts again.

"You don't have to say it," he murmured, assuring me. "I felt it too."

And with that, it was all I could do just to let myself get lost to him once more. I knew this wasn't the deal that I had made myself, but how could I resist? If I was telling myself that I was never going to have this again, then the least I could do was enjoy it while it lasted.

We went to bed, and he fucked me again, and I came so many times that I lost count. My body was jelly beneath him, hopeless to his touch, and I let him tip me over the edge time and time again until there was nothing left but my body, his body, the way we could make each other feel. I had no idea how I had managed to keep away from him for this long. It felt ridiculous, looking back. But what felt even more crazy was the reality that this was the last time – even if he didn't know it yet.

But the time that we fell apart, both gasping for air, on the bed, I knew in my gut that it was time for him to go. I looked over at him and felt that sharp start in my stomach, the one that told me that this was wrong. How could I turn him out onto the street when he had just – when we had just-

"What are you thinking about?" He asked, clearly sensing that there was something heavy going on inside my head, and wanting to ease the weight of it. I shook my head.

"Nothing," I replied, but I knew it was a lie. I had to tell him. I propped myself up in my bed and wrapped the covers around myself, not looking him in the eye. If I just didn't look at him, then I would be able to make it through this unhurt, unpained. I could pretend that I was just reciting these lines and that they didn't actually have any meaning behind them.

"I think you should go," I told him, echoing my words from the first morning that I had spent waking up next to him. I could feel his body tense beside me, and I felt a swell of guilt. I should have told him up front that this was how it was going to be. Not let him believe that there was a chance for more here.

"What are you talking about?" He demanded. His voice was low and I could hear the hurt in it. I tried not to look at him, but my eyes were drawn inexorably towards him once more. I wished that I had the strength to just tell him to go, but I was weak – so weak in the face of what I wanted to say.

"I think you should go," I repeated myself once more. The words were wavering as they came out of my mouth. I didn't believe them, and I could tell that he had his doubts, too.

"Why?" He asked bluntly, and I finally looked at him. God, those eyes – those eyes did something to me that I couldn't argue with. I wished that I had the strength to tell him the truth, that I wanted him to stay, that every part of me was begging me to allow him to remain here next to me, but I couldn't.

Could I?

In the dark of this night, far removed from what the day might bring, I could be honest with him. Just this once. He had to know, he deserved to know. He had been so good to me, and I had to do the same for him.

"Joseph, I think I'm falling for you," I admitted. I could see his eyes shine with delight when I said those words to him. And I knew I couldn't take them back, not now that they were out there.

"Abi," he murmured, and he reached across and brushed a strand of hair out of my eyes. "You know I'm falling for you, too..."

"This was meant to be the last time," I confessed, blurting out the words before I could stop myself. "Really. I wanted to move on after this. I thought this could be – well, I thought we could both get each other out of our systems, you know?"

"You really thought that would work?" He asked, smiling with incredulity. I sighed and shook my head.

"I guess not," I admitted. Now that I had a little space from it, I could see that all of this had just been an excuse for me to get him back into my bed again. Under the guise of *doing better*, but still – all this had just been an excuse I told myself to make it so that he could come back and be with me once more.

"I was going to kick you out," I continued. "I thought that was going to be the end of it, I really did."

"It couldn't be," he replied, a fire in his voice; his accent came through sharper and stronger when he was being heartfelt, and I could hear that brogue on his tongue as he spoke to me.

"You know there's something here," he told me fervently. "I feel it and I know that you feel it, too. I should have been more honest with you, I see that now, but you can't deny it."

I pressed my lips together. I didn't want to deny it anymore. That was the main difference. Even though I knew it could be dangerous, I wanted the whole world to know about us.

"I can't," I agreed softly, and he leaned over and kissed me once more. And I thanked God that I hadn't gone through with kicking him out, because the thought of making it through the rest of the night without him at my side was suddenly more weight than I could bear.

Chapter Eleven

Our little secret

I COULDN'T BELIEVE THIS was really happening. I just couldn't believe it.

I had never in a million years thought that I would be the kind of girl who did something like this. I was the good one, always had been, not the one who...well, not the one who gave into her basest desires, and allowed them to get in the way of everything else that went on in her life.

But ever since that night with Joseph, everything had revolved around sex for me. I had never known anything like it in my life; I'd heard before that when women got older they came into their sexual prime, but I was sure that was just a myth married housewives told themselves so they didn't feel too old and used-up.

But now...well, now, I supposed, I was starting to believe it.

I had never felt so wanted before in all my life. I think that was what did it for me. Every time he looked at me, I knew what was running through his head, and it made me wild to think of being wanted so much. Other guys, they had treated me well, but not like I was some prize to show off every chance they got. Joseph, though? Joseph seemed to want the world to know about us. Which made things pretty tricky, given that I didn't want anyone to find out what was happening between us.

I had even kept my mouth shut around Mallory – it just seemed better to make sure I didn't have anyone at all to worry about when it came to this. Better to be on the safe side and keep it all wrapped up to myself. She had only gotten a glimpse of him on my phone, too, so I had every hope that I would be able to sneak what was happening between us right on by her. I had told her that I had spent the night with him like she had suggested, but I had figured that it was just best to go ahead and leave it there. No need for her to hear any more of what had happened. It would just have been too strange for her to wrap her head around, after I was so certain that things were over between us before.

When in real life, of course, things were just starting to really hot up.

He would come down to my place every chance he got – his place was small, he said, and scant, given that he spent so much time out of the city – and we would lock the doors and curl up in bed together and forget that a world outside existed.

It wasn't just sex, either – no, he would hold me and let me talk to him about everything. How work had been that week, the song I had gotten stuck in my head and hadn't been able to shake. The fact that the new coffee shop across the street from me had these special artisan roasts and I was so worried about messing up the names of them that I just avoided saying them out loud at all.

Of course, there was one thing that I had decided it was just better that he wasn't aware of. Everything to do with my fertility. He knew that me and my last ex had broken up because we'd had different ideas about what we wanted for the future, but I had declined to go into any more detail about just what those things were. It didn't seem important for him to know, not yet. I would have been assuming that he was interested in more than he had expressed interest in so far, and I was the last person who wanted to jump the gun. I needed to stay careful with him, make sure not to get too invested or too involved, not until I had made it clear what I wanted from him, and figured out, once and for all, what it was he wanted from me, too.

"Ugh, I'm sorry I can't spend Saturday with you," I told him, about a month after we had started our little affair behind closed doors. I was lying in bed with him, my head on his chest, thinking about the next weekend that was to come.

"If it wasn't for this school trip, you know I would," I assured him. "I know you don't get long back on the mainland..."

"Don't worry about it," he replied, brushing his lips over my forehead. He would be going away for a few days midweek, and then I wouldn't get to see him again till Monday, because I had this school trip to handle. Though I would much rather have been spending time with him. I had signed myself up for this trip all those weeks ago because I had been hoping that it would keep me busy over the weekend so I wouldn't be tempted to spend any more time with him, but here it was, getting in the way of the very same thing.

"I need to find some parents to help chaperone me, too," I groaned. "And nobody ever wants to do it, not really. It's always so hard to find someone who's actually keen..."

"I could do it," he replied simply, and I raised my eyebrows at him.

"You mean that?"

"My sister goes to the school," He pointed out, and I winced – that was something I tried not to think about too much, if I could avoid it.

"I could help you out," he offered, and there was such a simple kindness to his voice that I felt my heart twisting up with joy. I liked the thought of that. I knew that it might be a bit of a pain getting the paperwork in hand, but it would be worth it.

To my surprise, it didn't take much effort on my part to get everything sorted. There were so few people offering to help chaperone the class trip that anyone who was willing to was practically a holy grail. I texted Joseph to let him know when and where to meet me, and he replied with a smiley face and a promise that he wouldn't let me down.

I was taking my class out to the local museum – there was this one-time exhibition going on with re-enactors of the period of history we were looking at, from around the time of the battle of Culloden. Normally, I would have been stressed out of my mind getting everything together for a big trip like this, but with Joseph there to help out, all of it seemed a whole lot easier to handle.

We met at the school in the morning, and the couple of dozen kids that I was taking care of today were already milling around excitedly waiting for the day to get started. I counted them all in and out, made sure that I had all the permission slips and money in hand for what we were doing today, and headed out the door. I had one other teacher and another chaperone helping me out today, and they ushered the children out of the classroom and into the waiting minibus; we only had the one that served the entire school, and it was a little battered, but it did the job.

"Hey," Joseph murmured, before I could get out of the classroom to join them. He caught me by the arm and pulled me in towards him. I grinned. I knew that someone could catch us at any moment, but I didn't care. I just wanted the excuse to be close to him again.

He kissed me, softly, quickly, his hands on my waist, his fingers teasing playfully at the bottom of my shirt; I managed to pull back before he went any further, but damn, it took everything I had in me not to tell him to just keep going the hell on.

"We have to get out there and catch up with them," I reminded him with a grin, pulling back with a moment to spare before it reached the point of critical mass. He brushed his nose against mine.

"Whatever you say," he replied, and I knew that this was a challenge – he was challenging me to keep going, to play his game with him. And yeah, okay, I would have been lying if I'd said that I wasn't more than a little tempted by the idea. But I had to keep my head in the game as long as I was out here on this trip.

Well, that's what I told myself, anyway.

I did exactly as much as I needed to in order to keep everything ticking over. I sat in the front of the bus with Joseph, and he pressed his leg up against mine, the pressure and weight of it more than I could take; I had to keep getting up under the guise of checking on how the kids were all doing, but I felt like everyone could see through me. He put his hand on the small of my back when the bus hit a pothole and almost sent me sprawling. Did anyone else see the way that my cheeks flushed red as soon as I felt his hand on me? I hoped not. If anyone caught wind of this...

We got to the museum, and the kids soon scattered, leaving us to chase after them and get them all together again in time for the performers who were meant to be coming in. The museum was old and dusty and looked like it had last been updated around a hundred years ago, but I still liked it. There was something to be said for places like this, places that felt like they were part of the history they claimed to contain.

We managed to get the kids in the same room again, and me and Joseph and the other two took our seats in the back of the performance space and watched as they began to re-enact in front of us. Joseph wound his fingers around mine, a little secret just for the two of us to enjoy, and I couldn't help but smile. He wanted me to know that I was his. He wanted me to know that he was mine. Even at a time like this, when we were risking a whole lot by doing this in the real world, it was worth it.

By the time that the re-enactment was over and the kids had had the time to poke around the exhibits and artifacts, I was getting tired, ready to head home and catch some rest already. The kids were all buzzed on the pop they had been sipping on their lunch break, and I knew that their parents would hardly be delighted to get them back in such an overexcited state. But it was hard to care, not when I knew that Joseph and I had the whole evening ahead of us once this was over.

We drove back to the school in that battered-up minibus, and I carefully counted all the kids out and saw them off to their parents once again. They were sweet kids, they really were, and they thanked me for taking them out that day. I smiled and nodded and told them that it had been my pleasure, even though the only thing on my mind in that instant was how soon I could get out of here so that Joseph could drive me home and I could pull him back into my bed.

By the time that everyone was gone, it was just starting to get dark outside. I liked this time of year; it was still warm enough that you could actually get out and do things without freezing your rear end off, but it got dark soon enough that I could steal away under the cover of night to do anything I wanted to.

"You ready to go?" Joseph asked, and he put his arm around my waist as we headed for the door.

"Ready to go," I agreed. And, as he led me out into the cool early evening air, I realized it - I was starting to fall in love with him.

Really in love.

Before, I had known that there was something there, and I had tried my best to pretend that it wasn't. But now I could see it was blossoming into something powerful, profound, something that I wanted to let bloom in its entirety. The world around me was just starting to sink into Autumn, everything cooling and changing. But for me, things were just starting to heat up. Life was coming into my world for the first time in what felt like forever. It was hard to imagine that I had ever, for a moment, thought that being with him had been a bad idea; it was so obvious to me now that it was how it was meant to be. That I was meant to love him.

"What are you thinking about?" He asked, as he started up the car. I shook my head and smiled. I would tell him, one day, but I wasn't ready for it quite yet.

"Nothing," I replied. "Come on, let's get home. I want to see what bad stuff is on TV that we can laugh at together."

"Sounds perfect," he agreed, and he leaned over and stole a quick kiss before we pulled off into the night together.

I knew then that I was falling in love with him. I still knew, of course, that I shouldn't have been – that this was destined to end badly one way or another, given that he used to be a student at this school and that this town was hardly known for its open and accepting view towards anything, really. But I was falling in love with him, and I hadn't allowed myself to be in love for so long that it felt like there was nothing to do but let it happen.

And even when I had loved before – it had never been love like this. Not really. Not the kind that I felt deep in my guts, the kind that rolled up and out of me, unstoppable. Before, I could have walked away from the men I was involved with if something had really called for it, and yes, it would have sucked, but I would have survived it. With Joseph, I knew that it wasn't going to happen that way. If someone had told me that I needed to cut him out of my life for good, I would have pushed back, found some way to fight it. Because I was sure that he would have done the same for me in an instant. He might not have been the man I thought I would fall for, but he was the man I had, and now, I just had to find some way to make that work with the rest of my life. I didn't know what that was going to look like, but I would find a way.

"What are you thinking about?" Joseph asked, as we pulled up outside my building. I looked at him for a moment, and wondered if I should have come out and said it. It would have been out of the blue, for sure, but I was certain that he felt it too. If I'd said it to him now, said those three little words, I was sure that he would have returned it.

"Nothing," I replied.

No. Not yet. Not so soon.

There was more that I had to do before I let myself go that far, more that I had to share with him, more that we had to work out between us. But I knew, then, at the end of that day, that I loved him. And that there was nothing I could do to unwind that truth.

No matter how hard I wanted to try.

Chapter Twelve

Tick tick boom

All of it had been going too well.

Looking back, I could see that now. It was obvious, when I thought about it, that there was no way the universe was going to let me off with things this easily. We had been together, properly, for about two and a half months, and everything was so perfect and so smooth and so delightful that I should have seen that we were ploughing straight towards a wall, doomed to the impact whether we liked it or not.

It was funny, when I cast my eyes back over that time that we had spent together, it was almost like I could see a clock ticking above my head. Yes, all that time slowly slipping away, counting down to zero, counting down to the moment that we were going to be exposed to the rest of the world.

He had come around to visit me at the school, taking me by surprise; I had been hanging out in Mallory's room, gathering some stuff for the next day and using it as an excuse to catch up on some gossip, when Nina, the secretary, had ducked her head into the classroom to catch my attention.

"Abigail?" She asked. I glanced over.

"Yes?"

"There's someone here to see you," she replied. "Looks like a parent?"

"Oh, right," I replied, and Mallory waved her hand at me to let me know that I was dismissed. I headed out and back to my classroom, expecting to come face-to-face with someone worried about how their little one was doing in my class – but instead, when I opened the door, I found Joseph waiting on the other side of it for me.

"What are you doing here?" I squealed with delight, and I closed the door behind me, glancing over my shoulder to make sure that nobody had seen my overjoyed reaction to him coming in. Nina had only worked here a couple of years so she would have had no idea who he was, and that was just fine by me.

"I got back a few hours early," Joseph explained. "The weather was turning so we got shipped off sooner than we expected. I know that I was meant to be coming around to yours to have dinner tonight, but I just wanted to see you..."

"You know you're being silly coming down here," I play-scolded him, and he grinned and put his arms around me. When he touched me, any attempts that I might have been able to hold on to in telling him off just fell away. I didn't have it in me. I never would. I was just pleased to see him.

Little did I know, of course, that the timer above my head was about to tick down to zero.

He leaned down to kiss me and I snuggled myself against him happily, delighted to have a chance to get a few more hours with him. Every second that we spent together was something that I treasured with every inch of my being. I knew that he felt the same way. He had never said it out loud but he had never had to; he showed it in the way he held me, touched me, pulled me close.

And I suppose I got a little lost in the way it felt to kiss him again. I knew that it was dangerous to let myself get this close to him on school grounds, but how in the name of hell was I meant to tell him to stop when he just felt so damn *good?* He kissed me deeply and I sank my fingers into his shoulders and cursed the world that kept me so far away from him most of the time. But, I supposed, absence made the heart grow fonder and-

"What the *fuck?*"

The two of us sprang apart at once. It was a woman's voice. I prayed that it was Mallory, coming by to pick something up from the classroom. Even Nina, though I doubted that she would have sounded so shocked. But when I turned and saw who had caught us in the act, my heart started to pound and my head spun wildly.

Mary. Mary Mackenzie. Joseph's sister.

Joseph dived after her but she got to the door before he could get close to her. I clamped a hand over my mouth, my eyes wide. No. No, no, no, no. If she knew...

If she knew, it turned out, then it wouldn't be long until the whole world did.

He slept next to me that night and had to go back out to the rig first thing the next morning. I tried to talk to him about what had happened but he shut down any conversation of it before I even got close. It drove me crazy – I needed to hear him say that he had seen her too, that the two of us could get through this, but he didn't say a word. Not a thing. It was making my head hurt just to think about it.

He kissed me before he left, clasped my face in his hands.

"I'll find some way to figure this out," he promised. I prayed that he would. I wasn't sure I believed him. Wasn't sure that I could.

I practically snuck back into work the next day, feeling like something was about to spring out from behind a door at me and catch me out at any moment. Turned out, I wasn't too far off with that.

"Abigail, there's a Ms. Mackenzie waiting for you in the office?" Nina told me as soon as I was through the door. Her face was tight, her lips pressed together in a visage of disapproval. "She came in this morning to speak with you."

I took a deep breath. I had met Rhona Mackenzie at parent-teacher stuff a few times, and she had always seemed uptight to me. I doubted that this revelation would have done much to improve her standing in that regard.

I got someone to watch my class for me for the next hour or so, and headed down to the meeting room to see what the hell she wanted with me. I knew that this was going to be intense, I knew that this was going to be tough. I could do it. I could do it, no matter what. I had no clue what Mary had told her mother about what she had seen of Joseph and I, but I doubted that anything would put her in a good mood about the whole situation.

Opening the door to the office, I tried my best to gather myself. But I could never have prepared myself for the onslaught that came pounding down on my head as soon as I stepped over the threshold.

"I can't believe you'd dare to so much as show your face at this school!" She exclaimed as soon as she laid eyes on me. I quickly shut the door behind me, glancing around to make sure that nobody else had heard a word of what she was saying to me.

"Rhona, please-" I tried to stop her in her tracks before she could go any further, but my attempts to make things better only served to get her to blow her lid even faster.

"Don't speak to me like that," she snapped back to me, pacing the small space of the office like an animal barely confined to a cage.

"My daughter told me what she saw between you and my son," she continued, her voice shaking as she tried to contain her rage. "She said she saw the two of you together. And I have no reason to think that she would lie about such a thing. I can't think of any reason she would come up with something so sick and twisted about her own brother–"

"It's true," I admitted, figuring that through was the only way out of this. "I can admit to that. But – but you have to listen to me here. It's not what it looks like. We met outside of the school, I had no idea who he was..."

"There's no way that you didn't know who he was," she sneered, and the disdain in her voice was obvious. It made me shiver. She hated me, she really did hate me. I was a people-pleaser, and knowing that someone like this would hate me was painful for me to wrap my head around.

"I've heard of women like you," she continued, already too far gone for me to pull her back.

"Women like me?" I asked, fearful already at the thought of what that might have meant. She shook her head, glared at me.

"You see boys like that at your schools," she continued. "And you're smart enough not to make the move then. But as soon as you get the chance, you get them because they're younger and they don't know any better and they're not going to put up a fight against you."

My jaw dropped. Was she really accusing me of being some sort of predator? It took everything I had in me not to launch myself at her, and I was far from a violent person. I just couldn't stand the thought that she would really believe that I had tried to force him into this.

"Rhona, your son came to *me-"*

"I'll bet that's what you'd have him believe," she continued, her face bright red from the exertion she was putting into the anger. "But I know better. A small town like this, you couldn't have not known who he was. He was at this school when you were. You taught him-"

"I never taught him," I protested, wishing I had some way to prove my point in the here and now that she would believe. She shook her head and lifted her finger, ordering me without words to keep my mouth shut.

"I don't want to hear another word from you," she told me. "I had to speak to you in person to see if it was true, but it's obvious that my daughter didn't make this up. I'm going to get you fired. I don't want anyone else falling victim to whatever your twisted little games are-"

"I'm not playing any games," I pleaded with her, in desperation. "I didn't know who he was, Rhona. I wanted to call it off, but then he-"

"But then he was the one who pushed for it, was he?" She demanded. "I'll bet that's what you'd have him believe, for sure, but I'm not so naïve."

She took a deep breath, gathering herself, a mother bear coming out to protect her cubs. I wished I could tell her that they didn't need protecting, that I wasn't predating on her son. We were just together. I loved him. I hadn't been the one to hold back about the truth of where we had first seen each other, he had. But she would find some way to twist that into my lies and his truth, and there was no way I was going to give her any more ammo than I already had.

"You need to leave," I told her. It was the best I could do; at least I could take some time for myself, get my head around this, think of some way to explain this all away and pray that I could get through this misunderstanding.

"Oh, I'll leave," she replied. "But I thought you should know that I'm going to be putting in a formal complaint about you. I can't in good faith let someone like you teach at this school any longer. It's just not right."

And with that, she marched out of the office. As soon as the door closed behind her, the tears started to flood down my face. I could hardly feel them; it was as though I was utterly numb, removed from what was happening to me. I couldn't think. I couldn't feel. I could only panic, panic, panic knowing that everything that I had made such a precious part of my life was about to come crashing down around me, and that there was nothing I could do to stop it happening.

I begged off work the rest of the day and went home, pulled the covers over my head, and ignored all the calls that came in. I needed time to think. I didn't know if I could fix this, but if there was some way, some way I could pull it all together, then I had to try.

I had to make an effort. But...but what could I do?

If Rhona had her way, and she had never struck me as the kind of woman who would renege on getting it, I would be painted as a predator, some older woman trawling the halls for my next target as soon as they were out of the school system. Joseph was so far away from me right now, and all I wanted was for him to pull me into his arms and tell me that this was all going to be alright.

But that was what had gotten me into this mess in the first place. None of this would have happened if it hadn't been for him. I could have carried on with my life, gone without him, gone apart from him. I supposed that was the part that hurt the most. That this could all have been avoided if I had just been able to keep myself together. I should have trusted my gut when I had found out who he was, told him to hit the bricks and get out of my life because getting involved with him was going to be more trouble than it was worth.

There was still time. I could do that now.

I had to put space between us, and quickly – I had to make sure that everyone knew that we were no longer an item. I didn't have it in me to outright break up with him, but at the very least I could shut down whatever it was that we had going on, put it on pause for a while and hope that it would be enough. I had no idea if people would buy it, or if they would see through my scheme in an instant, but it was the best I could think of for damage control right about now.

And that was all I could do in the blowup that followed what had happened with Joseph. I tried to put space between us. I didn't want to, God knows I didn't, but it wasn't like I had much of a choice. I just had to make sure that nobody saw us together, that nobody had any good reason to attach us to one another the way that Rhona had.

People at school knew. Everyone knew. I took another day off work the next day, just to avoid the horror of going in and facing them. Even Mallory – fuck, even Mallory would probably be stung that I hadn't bothered to tell her what was happening between us. I wished that I had, now, then at least it would look like less of a dirty little secret. I wished I could reach out to her and tell her that it wasn't what it looked like, but it was too late for that. I had to live with the choices I'd made. Even if they scared me. Even if they had put everything that I had worked so hard for for so long on the line.

I had to hide from the world for now. I had to keep it between me and my head. I would have to get out of bed and face it soon. But for the time being, I just wanted to hide from it. And as long as I could, that was just what I was planning to do.

Chapter Thirteen

All eyes on you

I COULDN'T WALK DOWN the street without feeling eyes on me.

And okay, maybe I was just imagining things as worse than they were, but I was sure that everyone in this fucking city knew who I was, and that every single one of them was judging me for what they thought they knew about me.

Yes, Rhona had made an official complaint about me.

Which was to say, she had made my business everyone's business.

I couldn't believe she would take this straight to the school, especially since it involved her son, but she had no interest in listening to anything that either me or Joseph had to say on the matter. She was too busy out here ruining lives, not giving a good God-damn how she hurt anyone around her. Rhona was a woman on a mission, and that mission seemed to be mostly centered around how to make my life as difficult as possible.

"You shouldn't even be here," I told Joseph, as he slipped through the door of my apartment; he was just back from the rig, having caught up on everything that had happened, and he had come straight down to see me as soon as he'd had the chance.

"I wasn't going to leave you to deal with my mother all by yourself," he replied firmly.

"Why aren't you at your place?" I asked, and he shook his head.

"Because I know my mum is going to be there waiting for me," he replied. "And I don't much feel like talking to her right now. Not after what she's tried to do to us."

He pulled me into his arms then, and held on to me tight, and I buried my face against his chest and let the tears flow.

I had barely been holding them back for most of the time that I had been exposed for. Okay, I had managed to make it back into work, which had been something, but it had been hellish dragging myself through all of that and knowing that everyone was looking at me like I was some sort of creep.

"You know we can't spare you for all this time," Jonah, the headteacher, told me with a frown on his face. "You'll continue to work as we conduct the investigation. If we find any wrongdoing, then we'll have reason to let you go."

I closed my eyes. Let me go. I had worked in this place for so long, and now they were talking about getting rid of me. It wasn't fair, none of this was. I felt like I was going to scream. How could this have happened? How could I have let this happen? Why couldn't I have been happy on my own, instead of going out into the world and daring to fall in love with the wrong man the way I had?

Thank God, most of the children were young enough that they had no concept of what was going on, and they didn't judge me for what they thought they knew. It was a relief to be able to come somewhere every day and know that I wasn't going to have to explain myself to everyone around me. I was glad to have a little haven, somewhere I could come and know that I wasn't going to be strung up as the most monstrous bitch who ever dared set foot in the school.

Mallory, of course, was also there for me, which was something; she was hardly the most popular woman in the world for sticking by me, but she made it clear that she wasn't going anywhere.

"I'm sorry, but I think this whole thing is ridiculous," She told me, over a glass of red wine over at her flat late one evening. We would have gone down to the pub, but I didn't want to run into anyone who might have some opinions to offer on the way I had been living my life lately.

"What are they going to do in that investigation?" She wondered aloud. "Try and prove that the two of you made eye contact in the corridor for three seconds ten years ago and that proves that you were after him since he was in school?"

"I have no idea," I replied with a long sigh. "I don't know what's taking them so long. I thought that they would have it all in hand by now, but it seems like it's taking longer than they thought it would..."

"That's because Rhona's trying to push through for something specific," She told me, draining her glass and going for another. "You know that she must be seething about all of this to kick up such a fuss."

"But why do you think she's so angry?" I wondered. "I mean, it's just dating. It's not like Joseph has to tell her everything that's going on in his life."

"He's her oldest, right?" She asked. I nodded.

"Tell me if I'm playing amateur psychologist," She began. "But maybe she feels like she's losing him? First one of her kids who's really left home, especially with working on the rig, and then she finds out that he's found another woman around her age who's dating him. Maybe she feels like she's being replaced or something."

"I wish I could just get her to see that it's not happening like that," I sighed, and I put my head in my hands. "I don't want to be his mother. I just want to be..."

"His lover," She finished up for me, and even in the state that I was in, I couldn't help but chuckle.

"Alright, I think that we put a ban on that word from here on out, okay?" I suggested. "Every time I even think about it, it makes me cringe."

"Agreed," she replied, holding her hands up in apology. "What are you going to do now, though? Going to keep working? Take some time off?"

"I think if I take more time off then it's just going to give people more space to make up lies about me," I pointed out. "If I'm actually there in front of them then it's going to be harder for them to spin the bullshit and make it stick. That's what I'm hoping, anyway."

"I think that's the best idea I've heard all week," she agreed, and she touched her glass to mine. "Cheers to that. I know you're going to get through this fine, I know you are. No way they're going to let something like this get in the way of your career. You're way too important to them at that school, I know it."

"I hope you're right," I muttered.

"I know I am," Mallory replied firmly.

But I could hear the tiniest little waver in her voice, and I wondered if she wasn't just trying to be nice to calm me down in the face of everything that was going on.

It wasn't until a few days later that I noticed something – kids were sliding out of my classroom.

Not just one or two on sick days, as would have been totally normal. No. More of them. More than there needed to be. And unless that the whole class had been struck down by the same case of dangerous lurgy, then I was pretty sure...

When I was on gate duty later that week, it clicked into place. People were pulling their children from my class. Parents who were there to pick up their other kids came along with my students in tow. It was clear that they weren't sick. Just that they didn't want them to be taught by someone the likes of me – someone with my reputation. I tried not to let it sting me too badly, but how could it not? I was being painted as a monster, some awful bitch who exploited and used the people who were meant to be able to trust her the most.

No wonder these people didn't want their kids anywhere near me.

I managed to keep it together as long as I was still at school, but the moment that I got off, I went back to my place and wept into my bed. I couldn't believe this was happening. All of this had started because I didn't want to be alone any longer, and where had it landed me? Feeling more alone than I ever had in my life before. I couldn't believe it. I couldn't believe I had been so stupid.

Joseph slept over with me as much as he could, keeping away from his family; he didn't blame his sister, he said, because she could never have known all the crazy stuff that her ratting us out would have brought into her lives. It was his mother that he was mad at. She knew what she was doing, knew the weight of it, and she had gone ahead and done it anyway. Because she was angry at me. At her son. Angry at us for daring to fall in love with each other, and angry that she couldn't control what was happening between us.

Sometimes, I felt angry, too. Not just at myself, but at all of this. I was angry at Rhona, of course, for pushing all of this forward when she had no good reason to; if she'd listened to me, or spoken to Joseph first, she would have heard that her son had been the one to come on to me, that I'd had no real clue who he was before we had first gotten together. Sometimes, there was anger at Joseph – not real anger, but frustration, the anger that a man I loved so much came with so much excess baggage to his name. I wished that it could have been easy between us, and I supposed I was angry with the universe at large for not making it that way for me. I had already been through enough as it was; at what point did I get a break, did I get it easy? Was it ever going to be easy for me?

"You know I'm not going anywhere, right?" Joseph told me, as he lay next to me in bed an evening about a week after it had all come out.

"I know that," I promised him. And I did, I really did. I was glad to have him here, and I wasn't sure that I would have been able to make it through had he not stuck by my side so surely.

"I'm sorry that you have to deal with all of this," he murmured, pulling me against his chest. I closed my eyes and rested my head on him, feeling the thump of his heart through his chest. I knew that heart beat for me, and it was about the only thing that made any of this survivable. If he hadn't been here, then I would have given up by now, I was sure of it. How could I make it through when it felt like the whole world, every card on the deck, when it felt like they were all stacked against me?

None of this was fair, but at least my prize for surviving it was to have this man.

The students missing from my classes were bad enough, but it went further than just that. It didn't take long until the rumors of what was happening started swirling with more speed, and soon, people outside the school had stuff to say on what was happening.

I passed Damien, one of the dads who always used to hang out at the front gate and flirt with me, as he was emerging from Jonah's office; he gave me a look, and then swiftly averted his gaze, as though being seen interacting with me on any level would land him in more trouble than it was worth. My stomach dropped. No way that this was good news.

A few hours later, Jonah called me into his office; he was regularly checking in with me to let me know how things were going, and to hear my side of whatever had been brought in that particular day. But I got the feeling that I wasn't much going to like hearing what he had to say to me right about now.

"Abigail, I've been speaking to some of the parents who encountered you when you were on gate duty," he explained, before I'd so much had a chance to sit down. "And they said that you were often – well, often acting provocatively with the men?"

I stared at him for a long moment, before I finally sank into the seat in front of me. I couldn't believe this was actually happening. I hated that I had to even deflect these bullshit claims, but if it was what was keeping me from doing my job to the best of my ability, then I would make sure I did what I had to.

"What do you mean?" I asked. I remembered that look that Damien had given me. It was more than just protecting his own skin – I could see it now, he was embarrassed by whatever it was that he had said about me in here.

"Acting inappropriately towards fathers and other caretakers," he explained, checking the notes that he had made. "Does that sound familiar?"

"I didn't do anything of the kind," I protested at once. "I mean, I spoke to them, sure, but that was it, it never went any further-"

"Are you sure about that?" He asked, tenting his fingers and looking over the top of them at me. I just stared at him, open-mouthed, for a long moment. How was I meant to respond? When it came to doing gate duty, everyone flirted a little bit; it was just politeness, after all. But I couldn't say that now, not while I was under this amount of scrutiny. Everyone would just take that as an admission of my guilt. I hated that everything that I did now was some sick proof that I was a sexual predator out to pick up whatever men came into my line of sight.

Up until a few months ago, I had been firmly celibate, had nothing to do with men for years, and now this was all happening so fast that I hardly had time to wrap my head around what it actually meant for me.

"I'm sure," I blurted out, but the tone of my voice made me sound like I was making it up. I had to bite the insides of my cheeks to keep from continuing to talk and just digging myself into an even bigger hole.

Fuck. Jonah made a note of something on the paper in front of him, and I had to fight the urge to reach across and snatch it from him just to find out what it actually said about me. What were people saying? What were people thinking? How could they all view me this badly, this quickly, when I had poured so much love and effort into this job over the years?

"Jonah, you have to listen to me here," I told him, steadying my voice and trying to pull myself together; I knew that I couldn't walk out of here letting him think that there was an ounce of truth to whatever Damien had told him. Damien had been the one flirting with me, and he was probably just throwing this out there to cover his own ass in case his wife found out that he had been enjoying my company a little too much during the school run.

"I know how this must look to you, but I've never done anything like that," I continued. "I'm committed to this job. I wouldn't have been here for so long if I wasn't. I wasn't just – I wasn't playing the long game all this time. I met this guy and we got together and I had no idea that he'd even been to this school."

I fell silent again, and I stared at him, waiting for a response. He didn't hurry to give me one. My toes curled in my shoes, and I fought the urge to slam my fist down on the desk in front of me and beg him to listen to me. I knew it wouldn't have changed anything. Jonah had to take these accusations seriously; the trouble that he could land in if he didn't would ruin his career. But when he looked at me, did he see anything other than someone who had been falsely accused of something heinous? I wanted to know. I needed to know. These last few weeks, they had been an exercise in learning who truly stood by my side, and who was basically out here causing me trouble no matter how hard I pushed against it.

I had to go back to class after that and act like nothing was wrong, even though I felt like I needed to scream at the top of my lungs. Had all of this been worth it? Had it? I kept asking myself that, a million times over, until the words had lost all meaning inside my head.

And the truth was – the answer was yes. I loved him. I hadn't said the words to him yet, and I knew that now wasn't the time, but I loved him. I loved him fiercely and with a passion, I loved him more than I had loved anyone before in my life. I loved him like my life depended on it, and sometimes, these days, it really felt like it did.

He was there for me, without question, in the face of all of it. He made it clear that nothing that happened was going to draw him from my side. He spent more time than he should have beating himself up over not telling me the truth of where he knew me from sooner.

"If I had just told you about all of this," he murmured to me, as we sat on the couch; he had offered to pick me up from school, but I had turned him down. Last thing we needed was for anyone to see us together. It would just give his mother more ammo against us, and God knew that that was the last thing we needed right about now.

"Then none of this would have happened," he continued, his face wracked with guilt.

"None of this would have happened," I echoed after him. "I never would have even met up with you. We've never have gotten to know each other. Do you really think that would have been worth it?"

"Do you?" He replied, turning those soft, worried eyes on me. My heart ached; I wished I could tell him, a hundred times over, that I would have done it again in an instant. I wasn't sure that even then he would have begun to believe me. I got the feeling that it wasn't going to be as easy as that. He was heavy with the guilt of having been the one to put me here, but I needed him to know that it wasn't him at all. That I had made this choice once I'd known the truth, and that I would have made it again if he had asked me to. Because what I felt when I was lying in his arms, that was worth all of the pain and all of the suffering and all of the sadness that came with this. I loved him, it was that simple, and love was worth going through anything for.

Right?

"I don't," I promised him. Sometimes, at times like this, I could see just how young he was; how vulnerable he could be. It made me want to take care of him. But that was what love did, right? That was how it felt when you really loved someone, when you knew there would be nothing that the world could throw at you that you wouldn't take on. I was so lucky to have him and I wanted him to know that. Despite everything, I wanted him to know that I wouldn't have changed this.

I would have changed how everyone saw it, though, if I'd had the chance. I would have made it so that when they looked at us, they saw a funny story, not something that needed to be capital-A addressed by the school and apparently the community as a whole. It made me so mad to think about everything that we had been put through – and for what? Because we loved one another. Because we were filled with the kind of hopeless care that came when the only thing that mattered was the way the other person made you feel.

That was what hurt me the most. Knowing that this could be held up as something so wrong. I wished that I could find some way to put forth the way I was feeling about him to the rest of the world – God, if I could have just told them all how he made me feel, the way he made my skin feel like it was buzzing with energy, they would have understood then. If I told them that I had never felt alive the way I did when I was with him before, maybe then, they would let it happen.

And look, okay, yes, I knew that to some people this would have looked strange. He had been a student at the school, and that had happened in the time that I had been teaching there. But people were exploding it way out of proportion, making out like I had practically swept in when he had been in short trousers to make him mine. Sure, he might have noticed me then for the first time, but the same did not go in the other direction. I hadn't even been aware that he existed until the day that he had appeared on my screen, and I had felt my stomach twist with the thrill of seeing his face. I would never have known anything beyond that, had it not been for the fact that he reached out to me.

And now I loved him, and it seemed like everyone around us wanted nothing more than for us to forget about one another. But how could I do a thing like that? As I lay there in his arms, I knew that it wasn't an option for me, not even close. I could have tried a million times over to leave him behind and none of it would have worked. Because he was a part of me now, the same way that I was a part of him. Losing him would be like cutting off a limb, and I was so far removed from being ready to take that on, I knew there was no chance I would go there.

"I feel like I caused all of this," Joseph murmured, as he smoothed his hand over my head. "If I had just told you everything in the first place..."

"We can't think like that," I told him firmly. "We're here now, right? I don't want anything to change that. I don't want you to go anywhere."

He managed to grin at me, despite the severity of the conversation.

"And there you were, kicking me out the first morning after we slept together," he reminded me. "You remember that?"

"Of course I do," I replied, flushing slightly. "But that was different. You sprung that on me then. I barely got to know you first..."

"You felt that way?" He replied, lifting his head so he could look at me. "Because I was pretty sure that I was in love with you even back then."

The words made something stutter in my chest. He had never said the *love* word to me, and though I wanted nothing more than to say them back, I had to take a second to wrap my head around what had just come out of his mouth.

"And I still do now," he replied. "Love you, that is. In case it wasn't clear."

"It was," I breathed. It had been so long since someone had said that to me that I had almost forgotten how I was meant to react. I smiled first, giggled, felt a little giddy, like my head was going to pop right off there and then. My brain was all fizzy, like it had suddenly been filled with carbonation. I propped myself up on his chest, looked him in the eyes, and spoke those words that I had been longing to say to him all this time.

"I love you, too," I murmured back. He cradled me softly in his arms, and slowly leaned forward to plant a kiss on my lips. It was a gentle gesture, one to seal our exchange of love, everything I needed right now.

In that moment, I could fool myself into thinking that everything was going to be just fine. Of course, I knew that was a lie; it seemed like the whole world was set against us right now, and there was nothing I could do to change their minds without just making myself look worse than I already had.

But I loved him. I loved him, and he loved me, and now that we had shared those words with one another, something solid had sealed between us. It didn't matter what his mother thought, or his sister – it didn't matter what the school imagined of me, what Jonah had to look into, what those men who had been flirting with me had decided to declare about my personality and the truth behind who I was. None of that mattered. Because we had each other.

I wrapped my arms around him and closed my eyes and tried to hang on to that feeling as tight as I could.

I knew that I was going to need to remember it. Whatever happened, it all came down to this – down to love.

And I wasn't going to let anyone on Earth take that love from me. No matter what.

Chapter Fourteen

Would you still want me?

"I DON'T KNOW IF I should talk about this stuff with you..." Mallory remarked, pulling a face where she sat opposite me at the coffee shop.

I grimaced. I knew how she must be feeling, but I had to hear this from her. Maybe I was just torturing myself needlessly, but I felt like I had to hear the words out of her mouth, to make me feel like I had any connection at all to the life I'd lived before.

"Just tell me what's going on at the school," I pleaded with her. "It doesn't have to be anything to do with me, really. I just want to know that everything is running as normal, right?"

"Right," she replied, eyeing me with some obvious nervousness. "Are you sure you're up to hearing this? I don't want to let you get down on yourself for no reason..."

I sighed and sank back in my seat. These days, I wasn't sure that it was so much no reason. I had managed to convince myself, for better or for worse, that all of this was just what I had deserved. After all, I had been the one to sleep with Joseph, even after I'd known what he was to me – I had been the one to fall for him. I had been the one to invite him along to that class outing. That was probably what had landed me in the most trouble, to be honest. People just assumed that we had been sneaking off and having sex in the bathrooms while the kids run amock with pointy objects and lit candles, and nothing I could have said was going to change anyone's mind. Everyone had already decided what kind of person I was, and that person certainly wasn't allowed anywhere near their children.

I wasn't sure how I was ever going to be able to go back there. Thing was, it wasn't even the kids that I was worried about – they had no idea what had happened and even if they had I doubted that they would have cared much, too young to bother with thinking much about the vestiges of adulthood that came with being a grown-up and everything that they might mean. But the thought of standing around at the gates with those parents, knowing that they were all judging me – no, knowing that they had all already judged me and that they were ready to write me off for good...it was that I couldn't cope with, not a moment of it.

The damage had already been done now.

Mallory was probably risking a whole lot just by being here with me, though she had been the one to stand at my side the whole time during all of this without a word of questioning as to where all of this had come from. She was a good friend, the best, and I wondered if she was nervous about being seen with me now that I was persona non grata around the entire school system in the area, it seemed.

"There's nothing going on there, anyway," she told me gently. "Nothing that really matters."

"I guess life's pretty boring without me there, huh?" I remarked, trying to play all cocky and fun, but it sounded more like the air being let out of a balloon. I wished I could have gathered some of the confidence that I had put together since I had been with Joseph, but it felt like all of that was just uselessly leaking out of me at every turn. I had wanted to change my life, to change everything about the way I lived, but this was hardly how I had expected it to go down.

Mallory sat there for a moment opposite me, and there was something to the way she was looking at me that raised questions in my gut.

"What's wrong?" I asked, and she shook her head.

"No, no, it's nothing-"

"Come on, the last thing I need is anyone else keeping secrets from me," I told her bluntly. "What's going on? Is everything okay?"

"Yes, it's fine," She replied at once, on instinct, the way all the women I knew had been trained as long as they could remember to just soothe anyone who asked for their soothing. But then, she flinched, as though that was the last thing she had wanted to do.

"Actually, I did just need to ask you," she confessed. "I mean, I trust you, I do, but I never – we never talked about this specifically..."

"Mallory, we've been friends for years," I reminded her. "You can just come out and say it, whatever it is."

"Did you know who he was? Before you got together with him the first time?" She asked.

I stared at her in silence for a long moment; I could hardly believe she would so much as think me capable of something so heinous. I didn't want to get mad at her, that would achieve nothing, but the sting of knowing that she had begun to question it was enough to make my stomach turn. She was the one who had been on my side all along, and now she was beginning to question that. How could I expect anyone else to stay solid and true when even the best of my best friends couldn't?

"I didn't know who he was, Mallory," I told her, and there was a pleading edge to my voice that I hadn't intended to have there. "I didn't, really. I never knew – if I'd known, I never would have done anything with him."

She must have heard the pain in my voice, because she reached across the table and took my hands. She squeezed tight, looked into my eyes.

"I'm sorry," she murmured. "I just...the way everyone has been talking since you left. I had to know. I had to hear it from you."

I let my head lower down and close my eyes. Everyone had been talking. So much so that even Mallory had started to question what she knew about me. When I had been going for the complete new start, this was hardly what I'd had in mind.

"You know I trust you, right?" She promised me at once, as soon as she saw the pain that was written on my face. "You know that I trust you. I just had to know. I had to know so that I could remind myself of that every time I heard someone talking..."

"So you hear them talking a lot, huh?" I asked quietly. She winced, and then nodded.

"I do," she admitted. "I don't think...I don't think you should come back yet, Abi. I don't think it's time."

Those words weighed heavy on me. I wanted to return, of course I did, but how could I do that when everything was just so *fucked?* I didn't know what I could do to try and convince the people who mattered that I wasn't some harlot out here trying to get with students as soon as they were old enough to walk out of the high school with a diploma. I hated that that was how I was viewed now, and I couldn't imagine getting out from under the weight of that name, of that title, of that reputation. If there was one thing that this town was known for, it was holding on to the past. You didn't get to just let go of what you had been before. People who had moved here twenty years ago were still called *incomers.* The history that you left behind, it wasn't so easily gotten rid of.

Joseph had been off at the rig for a couple of weeks, and that had left me with a whole lot to handle by myself. I supposed it was good, in some ways, not to be able to lose myself in him and forget about all my problems; I had to face up to what was right there in front of me, and God only knew how badly I needed to do that. But I wanted to bury my face in his chest and have him hold me and tell me that everything was going to be just fine.

The thing was, it was hard not to connect this back to him at the end of the day. I didn't want him tied up in these thoughts inside my head, but the truth was, he was part of them – he had been the reason for all of this in the first place, and escaping that truth wasn't going to be easy. Sometimes, when I thought of it, something stirred in me, some mixture of anger and love and guilt and worry, the fears that I would always hold these feelings towards him and that moving on from them was going to be impossible. I couldn't handle losing him on top of everything else. I had lost enough so far already, and the thought of having to let go of him too – well, it just made all of this seem even more useless.

But that time by myself, it gave me the space to come to terms with the fact that I was going to need to hand in my notice.

I couldn't stay at the school, not really. I couldn't go back there and be wracked with the judgment of the people who wouldn't so much as let their children around me any longer. The thought of living a life like that, it was too much for me to bear; I had to go out and start over somehow. Even if the investigation that they were carrying out came up with nothing, which I was totally sure that it would, the memories would linger long in the heads of the people who I was going to have to be around as long as I stayed there.

If it had been enough to get inside Mallory's head, then it would be enough to have them questioning me for the rest of my life in that school.

I cried the day I handed in my notice. I didn't want to leave. That place had been my home for so long, the thought of letting it go actually hurt me.

"Are you sure this is what you really want?" Jonah had asked me, when I had come into the school under cover of the sports day to give him my notice. I didn't want anyone to pay any attention to me being there; the fewer people that saw me, the better. I ached as I walked past my classroom, which had been run by a substitute, Mallory had informed me; apparently, she was good, but not nearly as good as me. But then, what else was my best friend going to say about her? I nodded to Jonah, gathering all my strength.

"Yes, I am," I replied. "I can't come back here, Jonah. Not knowing that all of you thought I was capable of doing something as awful as that."

He winced. He knew that I had a point. They had done something that I would never be able to get past; they had believed that I was some predator, out to collect the pelts of the boys who came through those doors.

"Besides, you really think most of those parents out there will be happy with the thought of me around their kids?" I pointed out, gesturing to the window, where the sports day was taking place. The sounds of their shrieks and laughs were enough to make my heart ache, but I managed to hold myself together. I didn't want them to know that this was hurting me as much as it was. There was still something in my guts that told me to have some pride. If this was a break-up, and that was just what it felt like, then I had to make like it was my choice to come through and be the one to end it.

"I know," He agreed. "But I believe you, for what it's worth. I wish that gossip didn't stick so badly in places like this. You know that I would have kept you on, right?"

I smiled at him. That was good to hear, at least – someone still had my back.

"And if you need a reference for anywhere else," he continued. "I'll be more than happy to provide it for you. With no mention of all of this."

"Thanks," I replied, and I meant it. I was so choked up that I couldn't come out with anything more effusive, and I knew that I was going to have to make it out of there before I started weeping right there in the middle of his office. Jonah was a good man, but he was also one who had little clue how to react to emotion, and he wouldn't have had a clue what to do with me.

I bid him farewell and made it back to my car before the tears really started to fall out of me. I wept in the car, trying to hold myself together, trying to figure out what came next, but nothing came to mind. I knew they always said that you shouldn't look back, but it was impossible when what lay behind me was still what I wanted, so badly. How could what was to come be better than that?

Joseph was back the next day, thank goodness, so I would have some company to keep me sane. I wasn't sure that I would have been able to make it through if it hadn't been for him. By the time that he came to my door, I was ready to fall into his arms and just let him hold me while I cried all of this out of my system and tried to scrub it free. I was ready to let go, to move on, and I knew that I was only going to be able to do that by pushing through the tsunami of emotions that were controlling me in that moment.

But when I opened the door to let him in, I was greeted by his smiling face. Smiling? What was he smiling about? I had told him what I had done, and I would have expected him turning up with a bottle of wine and a hug ready and waiting for me.

"Abigail, there's something I have to tell you," he began with excitement, and he kissed me on the mouth and stepped into my flat. I watched him in total shock; I had no clue how I was meant to react to this.

"What's going on?" I asked, voice tiny. I hadn't had much cause to use it since I had quit my job, and it felt dusty, like there were weights attached to it.

He sat down on the couch, and held out his hands for me; he pulled me into his lap and I landed there with a slight squeak of surprise. I couldn't help but smile. When he had me in his arms, I could fool myself into believing that everything was going to be just fine, even when it was such a huge mess.

"I got offered a new job," He explained. "In Orkney."

"In Orkney?" I replied, my heart dropping. If he had to move all the way out there, then we would be so far apart – seeing each other was hard enough as it was, I didn't want him to go anywhere else.

"It's an engineering job, so I won't be out in the middle of the sea most of the time – it'll be a nine-to-five, an office," he explained. "I'll be able to be close to home all the time."

I stared at him for a moment. I still didn't quite understand what he was getting at. Was I being stupid for not keeping up? I sat there in silence for another moment, waiting for him to go on, to shed some light on this.

"I want you to come with me, Abigail," he told me, finally, once he realized that the pieces weren't slotting into place for me the way he had expected them to. He took my hand and lifted it to his mouth, closed his eyes, and kissed it softly.

"I want you to come with me," He repeated, his eyes soft and his words certain. I had heard him the first time, but it was taking a moment for me to wrap my head around what he was saying to me in that moment.

"You want me to...?"

"I want you to come out there with me," he explained. "I don't want to leave you all the way back here. You said that your boss would give you a good reference, right? So use that, get a new job out there, a new start. With me."

My breath caught in my throat. I wanted to tell him *yes,* a million times over until the word had lost all meaning, but there were things that he needed to know about me before I could let him commit to something like that. He might have loved me, and I knew and was sure of the fact that he did, but he didn't know everything about me.

"What's wrong?" He asked, sensing the reticence from my side of things. I closed my eyes and buried my head into his shoulder, wanting this moment to last forever so that I didn't have to go ahead and tell him what came next.

"You don't want that?" He asked. "We could go out there together, leave all this behind – get a house, get jobs, start a family..."

I lifted my head from his shoulder and looked at him. This man, this perfect man – he had brought a perfect storm with him, of course, but out of it I had gotten him and I wouldn't have changed that. I reached out to touch his face, trying to calm myself, but the look in his eyes was nervous and I knew that I was going to have to come out and tell him the truth. The truth that I should have told him a long time ago.

"I want a family with you, Joseph, I really do," I promised him. "But I can't..."

I trailed off, caught myself, pulled myself back, I could do this. I had to say these words to him. He had to know what I had kept from him. It was only fair.

"I can't have children of my own."

He stared at me for a long while, like he could hardly get his head around what I was saying to him.

"What do you mean?" He asked softly, after a long silence.

"I mean, I'm infertile," I admitted. The words tasted like ashes in my mouth, and it took everything I had in me not to spit out the taste of them from my tongue.

"I'm sorry, I should have told you sooner," I went on, the words tumbling from my mouth. I needed him to know that I knew that I had messed up, to know that I understood that keeping this from him all this time had been the wrong thing for me to do. I should have been honest from the start but I had kept it to myself, frightened that everything that I was giving to him would be too much for him to take.

"But I didn't know what to say and I didn't even know if that's what you wanted from me," I continued, the words coming faster and faster until they threatened to blur into one another entirely. "I didn't want to assume, but then you...and I just couldn't..."

I lowered my face into his shoulder again, and tried to calm myself. I wasn't doing a very good job. I was just so scared that he was going to take one look at me now and walk away. There was too much baggage for him to carry with him into this new life that he was starting. He might have loved me, but love only went so far, and there was only so much that I could expect him to take as part of that love.

But then, I felt his arms wind around me again, and he pulled me close. His grip was strong and sure and a promise that he was never going to let go of me, no matter what. I looked at him, slowly, worried that if I moved too quickly I might do something that would blow all this up.

"I don't care about that," he told me. His voice was low, quiet, but it was certain. I stared at him.

"But how can you...you just said you wanted to start a family..."

"And there are plenty of ways that we can do that without having to get you pregnant, aren't there?" He pointed out. "You knew a lot of kids in that school who came along through – well, through routes that weren't the most traditional. And did their parents love them any less? Did they feel any less like kids to you?"

I smiled at him, even though the tears were still threatening. I shook my head.

"No, they didn't," I echoed, and he tightened his grip around me.

"Abigail, I love you," he told me. "And I love everything that comes with loving you. It's that simple. There's nothing you could tell me now that would scare me off, I want you to know that."

"Hey, don’t try me," I joked, and I managed a slightly shaky laugh. I couldn’t believe this was happening. My man, my man was still here, even though he knew that I would never be able to give him that part of myself.

Once I had gathered myself, I looked at him, deep in his eyes. I needed to know that he understood what he was getting into with this. I needed him to be certain.

"You know, this is the reason that my ex and I broke up," I told him. "The baby thing. And I know that you love me, but I don’t want you committing to something that you don’t fully understand yet and then getting hurt later down the line-"

"Hey, now," he protested gently. "I might be young, but I know what I want. You should know that by now, shouldn’t you?”

I smiled. It was hard not to. When I was here in his arms, it was impossible not to feel that wave of utter joy, of utter contentment. I didn’t know what it was I had done in a past life to make it so that this glorious man had chosen to be with me above all the other women in the world that would have long-since fallen at his feet and vowed to give him anything he wanted, but I owed that previous version of myself a thank-you.

"I want to go with you," I told him. "I want all of that. I need to get away from here..."

"We can have a house to ourselves," he murmured, his nose nuzzled into my neck. "All to ourselves. A garden, where the kids can go out and play..."

"Pets," I suggested. "I want pets, too. I haven’t been allowed any here."

"All the pets you could possibly want," he agreed, and he kissed me and pulled back and looked into my eyes.

"What is it?" I asked, feeling a little flush run up my cheeks. Sometimes, when he looked at me like that, it felt like everything in the world had slowed down around us; like everything was just taking a quick break, with every intention of coming back later, but for now, it was just the two of us, alone in the universe.

"I just can't believe I actually got you," he murmured. And with that, he kissed me again – and this time, I knew that it wasn't going to just end there.

His hands were strong and sure as he cradled me close, and his tongue parted my lips easily as he sank into the kiss. It was the start of something new, I could feel that. Not just that I had left so much behind, but that there was so much still ahead of me to experience, so much for me to know. Jonah would help me get that next job, and in the meantime Joseph would be there to guide me through every step of the way. And as long as he was here, well, I couldn't think of much better in the world than that.

He slowly lowered me back onto the couch, and let his full weight down on top of me. I could distantly remember, though it felt like a lifetime ago now, that I had convinced myself that I would be able to get over him with a single fuck – looking back now, that just seemed utterly crazy. I could never let this man go. He was mine, he belonged to me, and I belonged to him, and everything that we had been through together had only drawn us closer together and stronger than any couple I had ever known before. Yes, we might not have been the most conventional in the world, but that didn't matter. I was beginning to understand that convention didn't much matter when you carried with you the weight and the comfort of love, of being loved and loving right back.

He cupped my face in his hands and smoothed his thumbs lightly over my cheeks, as though marveling at the magic of having me right there underneath him, where I belonged. I smiled into the kiss as he parted my lips with his tongue, deepening this, taking it further, to where we both needed it to go. Before, sex had been an escape from everything that was happening, but now it was a gift; a gift that we gave ourselves and each other in equal measure. A pleasure that we owed each other.

He slipped his hand down and between my legs, pushing up the hem of the skirt that I was wearing and cupping my pussy through my underwear; I remembered the first time with him, when I had taken him to my bed after knowing him in person for just a few hours. I could vividly recall the questions I'd asked about whether or not this was a good idea, and how easily I had dismissed them when he had kissed me outside the flat.

Joseph slid down, kissing my neck, my collar, my chest, slowly unbuttoning the blouse that I had been wearing and pushing it open; he continued down, over my bra, my belly, my navel, lower, lower, lower, until there was no space left between his mouth and my underwear. He ran his tongue along the shape of them pressed against my skin, and I couldn't help but let out a moan of delight at the mere sight of him teasing me like that. He knew just what he did to me and he enjoyed every second of it, and knowing that this was stirring him to hardness the same way it was softening me to wetness was getting me so hot I could hardly bear it.

"You smell so good," he murmured, and he kissed the corner of my hip again before he looped his fingers around the fabric and slowly slipped it down over my hips.

He let out this soft groan as he exposed me like that; I loved the sound he made when he was hot for me, when he was ready and heady with the need of everything that I was giving him. I arched my back a little, pushed my hips back towards him, and the puff of pubic hair on my mound grazed over his skin. He looked up at me, his eyes burning with want, and he roughly pushed apart my thighs and lowered his mouth between my legs.

When he went down on me, it was like he wanted to feast there all night long; I cried up as soon as I felt his tongue against my clit, so familiar now, but just as amazing as it had felt the first time he had done it. I reached down and ran my fingers through his hair, pulling him on to me like I couldn't handle waiting a moment longer, and he grasped my thighs to keep me in place and lowered his tongue down to my slit. He pushed himself inside of me, and warmth and wetness of his soft tongue as he slipped inside me made my head explode into a chaos of stars and sensation and more than I could take in or take on. My hands fell to my sides once again, clutching at the couch for support, and my mouth opened and closed as I tried to find the words or the sounds to express how he made me feel.

He replaced his tongue with his fingers, and focused his oral attention on my clitoris once more; I lay there and let him pleasure me, unable to think or move or speak, struck dumb by everything that he was doing between my legs. Every now and then, I would look down and watch him between my thighs, remind myself of the fact that yes, he really wanted me, and yes, this was really happening, and yes, he had heard all those dark parts of me and accepted them at once. There were no more secrets between us now, nothing that I had to worry that he would reject me for. We had been through everything and come out the other side stronger and surer for all of it. I knew that nothing would pull us apart now, nothing could even come close to trying.

I felt that stirring, lusty need between my legs, as he sealed his lips around my clit and began to suck and lick softly. Every inch of my skin was prickling, and I smiled and tipped my head back against the soft cushion behind me as I felt myself edging closer and closer and closer...

He let out a long groan, and that was it, that was all I needed. Knowing that he was getting off on this just the same way I was tipped me over the edge and I came. It was the vibration of the sound that he made, as though I could feel it deep inside of me. Like he could speak himself into me, and I would hear every single word of it. I pushed my hips against his face and held them there, feeling the softness of his mouth up against me, letting myself get lost to it. The whole universe had narrowed to only include the two of us, and there was a hopeless bliss to letting that sweep through me, control everything.

By the time that he pulled his mouth away from me, my belly was rising and falling swiftly, and I knew that I needed to feel him inside of me. I needed that fullness, his body inside of mine; he seemed to sense it, and pulled me up onto his lap. I didn't even think about slipping on a condom. I didn't want anything between us, anything keeping us apart.

He unbuckled his jeans and wrapped his arms around me, gripping me by my hips and slowly guiding me down onto his straining erection. I gasped as soon as I felt him push into me – that sensation, that feeling, I was never going to get tired of it. To be filled like that, had, taken, and to give myself to him just the same way.

"You feel so good," he murmured to me, and he slipped his hand over my back and grasped the back of my neck, his hand on the line of my spine, drawing me close, driving me down on top of him. He held me steady as he thrust up and into me, going hard and slow, letting me get lost to the feeling of his body against mine. I gripped my thighs either side of him and rocked back and forth, leaning back so that I could look into his eyes and marvel at how beautiful he was when he was fucking me. His eyes were a little glazed, his mouth parted, but I knew that I was the only thing on his mind.

We moved like that for a while, taking our time, taking it slow, until there was nothing left to say or do but come; I could see him holding back, making an effort not to finish until I had come again, and I giggled and traced my finger down the V of his shirt, the fabric straining against his strong chest.

"I want to feel you cum inside of me," I murmured to him. And that was all he seemed to have been waiting for. I felt his cock twitch inside of me, and he filled me up; I felt like I was fulfilling some addiction, the relief of feeling him finish inside of me enough to push me over the edge again myself. My pussy clenched around him, as though clutching hold of him, and I gasped and buried my face into his neck to let the rush of it course through me. There was an intimacy to this, an intimacy that I never wanted to let go of when it came to him. He slowly drew himself out of me, lifting me from his lap, and I flopped down on the couch beside him and sprawled there. He ran his hand over my thigh and laughed.

"Good?" He asked, and I nodded.

"More than good," I agreed, and I closed my eyes and let my head rest back against the arm of the couch behind me.

"I'm going to get you a glass of wine," he told me, but his voice sounded distant, distracting. I nodded, managing that, at least, and listened to his footsteps as he walked away from me.

This was really happening. It had been sealed with a kiss now – well, with a fuck, really, if I was being honest with myself. But he wanted me with him. He wanted me to come to Orkney with him. And yeah, okay, that did scare me more than a little; the thought of starting over somewhere new after so long committed to this way of life was hard for me to wrap my head around. This was hardly the change that I had expected when I had embraced all of this, back then, back at the start of the summer when all of this had felt so exciting and new and necessary for me to move on.

But this was what I had needed. I had needed to meet someone like Joseph, someone who was going to change the way that I approached the rest of my life. Someone I had to break my rules for. It was scary, sure, but scary in the best way possible. I would have just dismissed that all before, told myself that the life I was living now was perfectly fine and that getting in the way of that was only going to make things worse. I would have stuck with what I had been doing, for fear of trying something new.

Joseph returned with the glass of wine for me and handed it to me as he sank down into the couch beside me.

"You planning on putting on clothes anytime soon, or...?" He asked, trailing his fingers over my bare belly. I shook my head.

"Nope," I replied cheerfully. "Don't see any reason to."

"Well, if you want me to get through this without getting distracted," he murmured, and he leaned over and kissed me. I smiled into the kiss, letting the taste of the wine on his lips and of me on his tongue sweep me away once more. So much had felt out of my control recently, but this, being with him, this was totally and utterly mine. This made me feel powerful, wanted, as though nothing could shake me from the space that I was taking up. And I never wanted to lose that. And, now that he had invited me to come with him to Orkney – I knew that I never would.

Author's Note

Was Abigail treated fairly? Would *you* send *your* kids to Miss Abigail's class?

Was Mallory a good friend? Should she have stuck up for Abigail more?

Joseph's mother hates Abigail. That's bound to be a thorn in their side for decades to come, isn't it?

Having spent some time in Scotland, what struck me most is how robust the Scottish people are. Historically, they have been the greatest of warriors and the most resilient of people in general.

The Scots are enterprising and have a remarkable ability to start anew.

For this reason, I believe that Abigail and Joseph will do just fine.

Read the next chapter for a look into their future together.

Love,
Viktor

Chapter Fifteen

Epilogue: You get what you need

THE AIR WAS COOL as it swept over the beach that morning; for once, it wasn't raining, though the trails of mist over the water threatened something different. For now, though, I would take what I could get.

"Hey, buddy," I murmured, and I leaned down to let Roe, our black Labrador, off the lead. He happily bounded across the sand, spooking a couple of the birds who had been minding their own business and pecking out some food from the sand. I grinned; those mornings when I didn't feel as bright or happy, my buddy could always lift my mood.

I paused for a moment, inhaled the air; when I had first arrived here, nearly six months ago, I had been able to taste the salt in the sky, and it had made everything feel so foreign and new and different. These days, though, I hardly noticed it. I supposed I was becoming a local. Fitting in. That was a nice thought, after all this time.

I could still remember, vividly, the day that I had told Mallory that I was leaving – it was the day that I had realized that everything had come together, the day that it had all become real as opposed to some fantasy I was hanging on to just for myself.

"You're kidding, right?" Mallory gasped. "You're moving?"

"Joseph asked me to come with him," I told her gently. I hadn't given her a pre-warning about the fact that I was going to head out of my job at the school, either, and I knew that she was still taking time to wrap her head around that. This must have been a bombshell.

"And you're going to go?" She replied, her eyes wide. "Just like that?"

I reached over the table to take her hand. She had been such a support in the time that I had needed her most, and the least I could do was try to help her through this now that I was going.

"It's not just like that," I promised her. "We've talked it over, so much of it. I know that this is what I want. I know this is what I need."

"Are you really sure about this?" She asked, clearly worried. "I don't want you to feel like you have to just...run away, now that all of this has happened."

"I'm not running away," I assured her. "I'm running *to* something. I know, I had to think about it for a while too, but I know this is what I want to do."

"But he's still working on the rig...?"

"He's got a job as an engineer now, somewhere closer to the shore," I explained. "So he's going to be around. All the time. We're going to live together, and he's going to-"

"You're going to live together?" She asked. It felt like everything I said, she was having to stop me dead in my tracks. I knew that all of this was huge, but seeing her reactions to it were just reminders of how huge they were.

"And we're thinking of starting a family," I confessed. This time, Mallory's face just lit up as soon as she heard the words come out of my mouth. She clasped her hand to her chest, utter delight, utter shock.

"Are you pregnant?" She asked, and I shook my head. I had never told her about the truth of my fertility. But in that moment, I saw no reason to hold back any longer; I had spent long enough in my life feeling like I had something to hide, but maybe this was a chance to unburden myself of everything that I had carried alone for so long.

"I can't get pregnant," I told her finally, after a long pause. "I...I've never been able to. That's why it ended with me and him before, because I couldn't have children. I never told you about it because I was ashamed, I guess..."

"Oh my God," she gasped, and she paused for a moment to gather herself. "I'm so sorry you ever felt like that around me. You know you can tell me anything, right?"

"I know that," I agreed. "I just had to come to terms with it myself first."

"So what are you going to do?"

"I'm going to look into adoption," I explained. "That's what we want to do. I know it's going to be a long process, but I want to start a family with him. Out there. I really do."

"Oh my God, I'm going to miss you so much," Mallory told me, and she suddenly dived over the table to give me a tight hug.

"Hey, I'm not going to be gone forever," I protested with a laugh. "And you know that when we do get these kids, they're going to need their auntie Mallory around to help take care of them, right?"

"Of course," she agreed. "And there's no way I'm not going to be there to take care of them any chance I get. I'm going to be the most obnoxious aunt the world has ever seen."

"I should hope so," I replied, and she pulled back and looked at me. She looked a little teary, but there was a wide smile on her face.

"I'm so happy for you," she told me, and I could tell that she meant it. "I know how much you've wanted this for so long."

"I really have," I agreed, and she squeezed my hands tight and I knew that she was behind me every single step of the way. I was going to have such a hard time moving so far from her, but I knew this was the right choice; I needed that time, that space, that ability to stand on my own. To prove that the life I'd had back here wasn't where it started and ended.

Of course, when Joseph's family found out that we were planning on moving away together, they instantly kicked up a total stink about all of it.

"You can't just run off with her!" His mother had exclaimed, once he had managed to coax her out for dinner with me as a chance to get to know me better. Joseph held my hand under the table, soothing me, reminding me that, no matter what happened, he was there for me.

"I'm not just running off with her," he replied, as patiently as he could, though I could tell that it was taking every ounce of restraint that he had in him to stay calm and not get angry at her. He didn't take well to people casting any aspersions on our relationship. We had already been through enough already, and the last thing he needed was his mother getting in the way of what we had.

"I'm moving out there because I got a job offer," he explained. "It's going to be good, I'm sure of it. And I want Abigail to come with me, because-"

"Because she knows she couldn't possibly get any work down here anymore," she replied with a sneer of distaste. I felt something jolt sharply inside of me. I wanted to tell her that she was wrong, that this industry wasn't done with me at all, but I kept my mouth shut. Any kind of reaction would be too much. She was looking for anything, any reason to jump on me that would prove that she had been right in everything she was thinking, and I was damn sure I wasn't going to give it to her.

"I wanted you to know before I went anywhere," he continued, calmly, ignoring what she had just said. "Because I felt like you deserved a chance to make your peace with it before we went."

"I have nothing to make peace with," she replied, shaking her head and leaning back from the table. "You can go if you want. I can't stop you-"

"We're going to have a family out there, Mum," he told her, and that seemed to bring her to a sharp, grinding halt in her tracks. She balked, something I had never seen someone do in real life before, but she managed to gather herself quickly and she eyed me.

"And this is her idea, I'd imagine?" She replied. "Trying to get you locked in before you know any better? Well, let me tell you, I think it's sick-"

"It was mine," he told her, cutting her off again. "I want a family, Mum, and I want you to be a part of it."

From that moment on, it seemed like something had shifted inside of her. I knew that she was still far from happy that I was going to be basically running off with her son, but there was little that she could do about it. And she wanted to be part of the family we were planning on having, too. There were a few stop-starts, a few back-and-forths as we tried to find our way through it, but she came around to me. Mary did, too, though I knew she still sometimes found it a little strange that her brother was dating someone who'd used to teach her. She didn't mention it, but I could see it on her face sometimes. They didn't come to visit us all that often, but each time they did, I could have sworn that Mary and her mother were getting a little warmer towards me. The last time, Mary had even baked a cake and let us all tuck into it together, and she had smiled broadly when I had told her how delicious I thought it was. That was the good thing about having worked as a teacher for so long, I supposed, I was good at dealing with girls like that.

Not to mention the fact that they seemed to love the little home that we had put together as much as we did. I'd had no idea what to expect when we started looking at places to buy in Orkney, but I knew I wanted somewhere big, with plenty of room, somewhere that we could raise a family all of our own. We went through a half-dozen places, traveling all up and down those misty, winding, wet little roads to make it to our appointments on time, but nothing turned up – until we found that tiny little spot near the beach, the one that just spoke to us as soon as we saw it.

"Oh my God," I gasped as soon as I laid eyes on it. It was a small cottage, the kind that seemed to cling to the side of the cliff that it was at the bottom of for dear life – it looked as though one sturdy breeze would have been enough to knock it into the ocean, but for some reason, I liked that. It was made with old, uneven flagstones, and looked out onto the beach below.

"At high tide, the water gets close to the house," The estate agent, apparently one of only two on the island and very pleased indeed to be able to claim our custom for herself.

"But that just means you'll have to keep your gardening to the side," she explained, as she guided us around the back and gestured to the little miniature paddock that would be ours right alongside this place. I beamed, and turned to look at Joseph. I could tell from the way he was looking at this place that he, too, felt the same way that I did for it.

"Could we take a look around inside?" I asked her keenly, and she gestured for me to lead on; the front door was a little warped, probably from all the cold and rain, but it reminded me that this place must have been around for so long. There was so much history here, far more so than my little flat back in Inverness.

By the time that we had made our way around the house, I knew that this was the place for us. It was small, just enough room for the two of us as well as a kid if we decided to have one, but I actually liked that – there was a coziness to it, a comforting smallness that made me feel like I would be able to get all of this under control. Joseph paused next to me in the bedroom, and I looked over at him.

"You feel it too, don't you?" I asked him, winding my arms around his neck. "You feel it too."

"Of course I do," he agreed, and he kissed me on the cheek. "This is perfect, really. I think we should put an offer down now."

"Now?" I squeaked back. "Shouldn't we take some more time to think about it?"

"I don't think you need to," he pointed out with a smile. "This is where you want to live, isn't it?"

I bit my lip and nodded. I was so grateful for him. I was grateful that he could look into my eyes and see what I wanted, see what was best for me, even when I was unsure about it. I needed someone like that, someone who was never afraid to strike out and take control and do the right thing. I loved him for this, for all the time and effort he put into understanding me, into making sure that I got every little thing that I wanted.

We put our savings together and bought the place at once, and by the time we got back to the mainland that night, I was officially the owner of my very first full-blown house. I couldn't believe it. I missed it already, even as I lay next to Joseph that night and listened to the slow rise and fall of his breath. How could I feel so attached to somewhere that I had never even lived in before? I could already feel it calling to me, like it was trying to guide me home. I wanted to listen more than I wanted to do anything in the world. I wanted to go back there already.

The move was a bit of a pain in the arse, given everything we had to load up into the cars to get them over on the ferry; but it was worth it. Joseph kept my attitude light and bright as we went, and he wound his arms around me from behind as we looked out over the retreating mainland in the distance. Like the both of us were silently bidding farewell to the lives that we had known there, for better or for worse.

I was surprised at how quickly I found myself settling into life on the island. I had assumed that it was going to be tough at first, getting used to the pace of things out here; I knew that I had a lot to get used to, given that my normal had been being able to go out and get drinks or food or anything I wanted at any time of the day or night. These days, I had to trek out to the shop in the tiny street near the ferry port to get everything, and I soon learned that I was foolish not to take a list because there was always something that I would find some way to forget.

It had been there that I'd met Marie, one of our closer friends on Orkney; she was a woman a little older than me who ran the shop, the one who had hold of all the town gossip, it seemed, and was willing to share it with anyone who came in. It was through her that we had met Roe, when he had been looking for a new home after his owner was called back to the mainland suddenly; she set us up with a meeting with him, and as soon as I laid eyes on him, I knew that he was the dog for us.

"Oh, can we keep him?" I pleaded with Joseph playfully. He grinned at me and got down on his knees to say hello to the dog.

"I think so," he agreed. "As long as you can walk him, alright? I'm not getting up any earlier than I have to for work in the mornings."

"Of course," I agreed, and I kissed him on the cheek. He already worked so hard for the two of us, and I was so grateful for it.

And as for my own teaching career – well, okay, it turned out that there weren't a huge amount of jobs going up in Orkney or any of the surrounding islands when I got there. But soon, I found myself settling into the pace of life just living off my savings. I thought that I belonged in the classroom beyond anything else, but now, these days, I was quite sure that there was more to my ability to share knowledge than that. Teaching in a classroom was an awesome thing, of course, but I would never look at it as the only way to pass on what I had learned.

I took up tutoring on the side, helping out the kids I worked with here and there, just about twenty hours a week all in. And it was a blissful thing, being able to make my own schedule like that, because it meant that I could focus on building this home for us the rest of the time. When he came home from working on the dock all day, I could have dinner on the table and be ready for him with a kiss by the door. I had never imagined that I would be the kind of woman who would find joy in something as simple as that, but when it came to taking care of him, I got such a great happiness and contentment from it that nothing else appealed to me any longer.

And yes, of course, we had started looking into raising a family of our own out here. We had promised each other that we would give it a year before we committed to anything to do with kids, just to make sure that we actually liked it as much as we thought we did, but now that we were six months in, I knew that he was thinking the same way I was about it.

Everything was so much easier out here. And not just because nobody knew about our background, the drama that had followed us when we had first started out together. There were fewer people in our lives now, and the ones that we chose to keep around had to make a specific effort to be there – Mallory, his family, our few friends that we had around the island. People couldn't just stop by to come and poke around and try and pick up on whatever gossip they had come looking for about the two of us. It was a relief, actually, to know that; to know that whatever we did, it wasn't going to be the center of some focus, but rather, the choices we made because we knew that they were the ones that worked best for us.

Adoption was a long process, but I had been prepared for that from the start. The fact that I had experience being around kids helped a lot, and the couple of meetings we'd had with social workers to get a scout out on our location, work, and general relationship had gone well; I knew that it was a tick in my favour, and I intended to make the most of it that I could. Sometimes, I felt impatient at the thought of having to wait any longer to welcome our first child into our lives, but then Joseph would remind me that everything good that had come to us, we'd had to wait for. This was just an extension of that. And our family was going to be the most perfect thing in my whole life; I wasn't going to hurry it along.

Besides, I had Roe for now, and I was just happy getting used to having another creature to take care of. He was a young thing, full of that puppy energy, and I knew that he was going to be the perfect protector for our little one, however old they turned out to be. Sometimes, I had trouble keeping up with him, but he would always pause to come back and wait for me to catch up. This was what it was like being surrounded by younger men, I supposed, you were constantly hurrying to keep up. But that kept my head focused firmly forward, not looking back, and I wanted that. I needed that.

As I stood there, watching Roe bounce around in the freezing cold water like he had never seen it before, I couldn't help but smile. A year ago, if you'd told me that this was where I was going to be then I would have been sure you were crazy. But now that I was here...well, it just felt obvious. As though this was where I had been heading all along. It was hard for me to believe that I hadn't, in some ways; that the universe hadn't been guiding me to this end. To him. To Joseph. To this. To the life that I wanted, but didn't know I needed until I had it.

Back at the house, I knew that Joseph would just be getting up for work. I liked to take Roe out early so that I could go back and have breakfast with him before he went out for the day. He worked so much these days, but I knew that he loved it; it just meant that I had to come up with smarter ways to feed him in the evenings, because he would be so hungry by the time he got back that he could have eaten most of the cupboards if I hadn't been careful. I called Roe to me again once I was satisfied that he had stretched his legs, and headed back to the house.

Sure enough, there was Joseph, boiling the kettle and yawning. He was wearing just a pair of jeans – the cold didn't seem to get to him the same way it did to me.

"Morning," He greeted me, and he leaned over and planted a kiss on my cheek, before getting down on his knees to say hello to Roe. I was pretty sure that dog loved Joseph more than he loved me, though Joseph had claimed to be less of the animal person out of the two of us. I wasn't sure I believed it.

"Morning," I murmured back. And, as I watched the two of them together, the beginnings of the family we were going to make with one another, I knew it.

I knew that this might not have been the chance that I had expected, or the change that I had wanted. But, above all of that, it had been the change that I'd needed. The change that had put everything in my life to rights.

I couldn't think of anything else, in that moment, that mattered more than that.

Bonus chapter

Excerpt from the book Shameful Addictions

"Enter," his voice called. When raised, it had a rough undertone.

Knowing she had no hope of preparing herself, Charlotte shoved his door open and thrust herself into his office.

The room unfurled around her, cavernous in size, lined with gigantic photographs and paintings of scantily-clad women in all sorts of scandalous positions. Backs were arched unnaturally, thrusting out their breasts and asses, which were all too large and perfectly round to be natural. Platinum-blonde hair, always platinum-blonde, spilled over their shoulders, down their backs, trailed over their rotund asses. Their lips were plump, unnaturally so, and shiny with makeup. Their faces were blank, lustful, high color in their cheeks as they arched and stared upwards.

Even in the paintings, those details were clear. The artists had rendered their models with hyper-realistic details,

Charlotte stood there, framed on all sides by the pornographic images. They showed her what this man was really like, what he really wanted of his women, as if she'd had any doubt. He saw all women as the same, all women as whores. She was another whore to him, too. A money whore, come to try and suck him dry.

Mamba sat far across at the other end of the room, in front of an entire wall of window panes, showing the city below. Shorter skyscrapers, office buildings, clusters of stores, strip malls, and the roads that wove through it all, covered in cars and rimmed with pedestrians; he lorded over it all like a king at his throne. He even wore the modern man's equivalent of king's clothing, an expensive suit tailored to fit his tall, muscular body.

"So you're smart enough to listen to instructions," he said, and gave a dry smirk that chilled her to the bone.

Charlotte clasped her hands in front of her and held her head high, trying not to show him that she was intimidated. She took a step forward.

"Don't come closer," Mamba said. His voice was still so smooth and measured and he still smiled, but it was an obvious command.

Charlotte froze where she stood, heart thundering in her breast. As much as she didn't want to, she had to obey him. Her future depended upon it.

Mamba folded his hands on his executive desk, smiling that unpleasant smile. "You aren't fit to approach me. Tell me what it is you want and be quick about it. While I'm wasting time with you, I fall behind on more important matters."

This is the most *important matter to* me, she thought. He had no sympathy for her. She hadn't expected him to and it was still disheartening to see for herself.

"Speak," he commanded.

She recalled how he had wanted her to beg before. It might well be her only chance, to appeal to his ego. She forced herself to lower her head and spoke while looking at the gleaming white expanse of floor. Her voice echoed across the vastness of the room.

"Mamba, I can't afford to keep paying you. I've done everything I can, but I'm absolutely broke. There's no more money left in my bank accounts. I've sold all my jewelry to reach last month's payment. Now there's nothing left. Please. I'm begging you. Can we come to some sort of agreement? You won't get any money at all if I go to jail for defaulting on the payments. Only you can help me."

Mamba suddenly started laughing as she finished. His shoulders quivered with an evil merriment at her expensive. His laughter cut off quickly and he leaned forward in his chair, glaring at her with his cold venomous eyes. "I'm sure you've noticed that hardly anyone dares speak my name. They seem to think talking of me will summon me."

That's how this happened to me, she thought bitterly. She said his name too many times and he came at the summons, like a ghoul, a demon, rising out of darkness to ruin her.

"From now on, you will address me as sir."

He didn't elaborate on what would happen if she didn't. He didn't need to. The implications were clear.

Charlotte lowered her head. "Yes, sir."

"Why should I prevent your life from being ruined when you attempted to do the same to me?" Mamba asked. "You tried to play a game in which you didn't know the rules. You brought this upon yourself. You played with fire. Whether you burn yourself is none of my concern. Do you understand? I don't care about you. Not at all. You're nothing. A worm. An ant. An annoying speck of dust."

Tears stung her eyes. "Then why," she whispered, voice trembling, "are you doing this? If you really don't care?"

"That's business." He lifted one shoulder in a careless shrug. "You are a demonstration of what happens when people try to mess with me. You're a tool. Unfortunately, you are a very old and outdated tool capable of only one thing. I can use you, but only this once. You aren't a real woman. You can do nothing more than this and soon your time will be finished. You'll be broken. And then you will go to jail with the other pieces of garbage."

Charlotte came to a realization while Mamba spoke. It was that one sentence in the middle that gave her true insight into the deeper meaning of what he was saying. She wasn't a "real woman" in his eyes. The fake whores, more plastic than person, lining his walls were what he considered to be real women. He wanted tools. He wanted big-lipped and busty females who would perform whatever task he wanted and fill every role he required of them.

Despite all his claims to support the empowerment of women, he had just revealed himself to her as a complete and utter misogynist.

If only she'd been wearing a microphone or had a recorder in her pocket, she could have recorded him and fought back.

Maybe he's right. I'm old. I don't know what I'm doing anymore. Maybe this is what I deserve.

She risked a glance up at Mamba and saw him grinning, gloating, more than likely able to read every thought that crossed her face. This was what he wanted, for her to give up, for her to believe what he said about her.

The urge swept through her to show him her middle finger and storm out. Fuck him. Fuck everything he stood for. She'd find a different, less degrading way to get through this.

"What are you considering?" Mamba's eyes narrowed to slits. He thrummed his fingers on his desk, the tapping echoing like gunshots in the cavernous office. "You want to pretend to be a bad bitch and storm out of here. How very noble of you to stick to your guns even in what is so clearly a desperate time for you. You'd have my admiration, except I can reassure you that you won't make it very far and you will get very little done. You've learned nothing from this whole ordeal."

"What am I supposed to learn? Sir," she added, lamely.

"That you are no better than any other woman. You are no different, though you think you are and so you have pigeonholed yourself. But you are not different. You think I can't tell you orgasmed recently?"

She couldn't have been more shocked than if he'd thrown a bucket of ice water in her face. She sputtered, "What... How..." She shifted her clasped hands, subconsciously covering her pussy. She'd showered. She'd put on perfume. He shouldn't know that she'd had an orgasm. It had to be a trick.

The confidence in his smirk told her that no, it wasn't a trick. He really knew. He could really tell. She may as well have been naked and standing in front of him with her pussy wet for all she could hide from him.

"I will write off one month's payment," Mamba said in his slow hiss. "This month's. You'd best do all you can to get back on your feet in that time."

She was too relieved to argue with him about how he'd ruined her reputation so thoroughly she might as well not have feet to stand on. He'd chopped them off, amputated her foundation.

"In return, you will dye your hair my favorite color."

His favorite color. Blue, like the sadness he inflicted upon others? Or red, like the blood of his enemies?

She was about to ask when it hit her. "No," she breathed.

"Yes. Platinum-blonde. You will do it and you will send me proof. No sooner and no later than I receive your proof, I will write off the payment you owe this month."

The same color as the girls in Club Lollipop. The same color as all these women rimming his office. Whore hair. Stripper hair.

Anger rose in her throat. "You can't be serious."

"You're angry. That's very funny to me, that you still have the audacity to be mad after all this." Mamba laughed aloud. "You must know that dying your hair will cost far less than what you owe me for this month. Even if you went to the best stylist in town."

He stopped laughing rather abruptly and leaned back in his chair, as if bored with her. "That is my offer. Take it or leave it. I, of course, don't need the money you owe me, but you do need this break. Are you going to be such an uppity bitch that you won't do it? Then go to jail. That would amuse me, to see you behind bars. I might have to visit you and see how you're faring. You will have to introduce me to whatever butch woman decides to use you as her bitch."

She absolutely couldn't believe this. But hadn't she said she'd do anything? This was her only way out. Damn the insufferable man for making sense. Damn him.

"Get out of my office." Mamba swiveled in his chair, ignoring her, gazing out at his view of the city.

"Yes, sir," Charlotte murmured. She turned and got out of there as fast as her legs could carry her.

What to read next

Read Now

https://books2read.com/shamefuladdictions/

Also by Viktor Redreich

Innocence Corrupted Collection

Trixie Provoked

Sophie Corrupted

Megan Disgraced

Amber Stigmatized

Cindy Violated

Kelly Exposed

Savage Satisfactions Collection

Submissive Nanny

Hunky Neighbor

Blushing Maid

Risky Mistress

Jealous Wife

Demanding Husband

Desires Unleashed Collection

Dangerous Desires

Indecent Temptations

Explicit Demands

Sordid Fixations

Illicit Compulsions

Shameful Addictions

Books can be read in any order

Get your free copy of Dirty Secrets

Elyse said that she's been secretly letting a young man fuck her. He's her massage therapist and he was supposed to keep it professional but his hands kept wandering under the towel and touching her in places he *shouldn't* have been touching her.

One thing led to another and pretty soon he just peeled off his clothes. Fit body completely exposed to her, he climbed up on top of her, pushed her legs apart, and penetrated her.

Elyse isn't the only one having fun with younger men. Nicole is too.

In fact, Nicole told me that the college guy who lives next door to her has been watching her sunbathe in her bikini by the pool. At first, she was angry about him staring at her from his upstairs bedroom window. Soon though, she started to enjoy the attention.

Last I heard she even took her top off and rubbed lotion on her titties for him to watch.

Oh and you who else is behaving scandalously? Miranda.

Miranda's husband is a hunk and their sex life is great. She heard her husband bragging to one of his friends about how good and sexy Miranda is. How willing and eager she is. How she's basically up for anything.

Then out of nowhere Miranda's husband told her to suck his friend's dick.

Do you think that's going too far?

I think they're *all* going too far. Elyse, Nicole *and* Miranda.

What shocks me is how eager they were to tell me these things. How much detail they went into.

They really opened up to me. They literally told me *everything.*

Being a writer, I wrote it all down. Every dirty detail. All of Miranda's, Nicole's, and Elyse's secrets, plus the secrets of many other women just like them.

Just like *you*.

Get your free book now

Redreich.com/DirtySecrets/

www.ingramcontent.com/pod-product-compliance
Lightning Source LLC
La Vergne TN
LVHW012051160826
845678LV00014B/2778

* 9 7 8 1 9 1 3 3 7 6 2 4 6 *